"I like it wh
willing," T

He moved his arm from around her shoulders to the swell of her breasts and traced his fingers over the sensitive curve just above the nipple. Immediately, Carrie arched her body toward him, demanding more.

Yes, she silently agreed—to whatever he wanted…anything he wanted…as long as he kept up his rhythmic stroking. He came behind her slowly, pushing into her hot center so that she felt every hard inch of him as he entered her.

Truck rocked against her gently, testing her need. She pushed back against him. Then he boldly grasped her hips and thrust into her, riding her hard, hot and heavy, mastering her soul.

Driving into her one final time, Truck felt his own climax coming. "Did you think what we had was over?" he whispered once he'd regained control. *"We're not done yet, you and I."*

Dear Reader,

I'm so excited to be a part of the Harlequin family! And I can't tell you how much I've enjoyed writing not only my first Temptation novel, but a story set in a part of the country I truly love: rural Maine. In creating the fictional town of Paradise, I tried to capture the spirit of the area where my husband's family has summered for many years—and truly portray just how special a place it is.

We spent our honeymoon there, and I will never forget my first impressions—coming down the interstate at five in the morning with the red sun rising and the air so bracing and cool. I have fond memories of those late afternoons spent on the porch of the cabin, just watching the pond and listening to the ducks and loons. This is where I wrote portions of three or four books, in the days when I still resisted using a computer.

But like Carrie, my heroine in *Night Moves,* I had to learn to love and appreciate the time I spent there. Now, for me, it has become both a place I long to be *and* a state of mind. I hope my readers will feel that way, too.

All my best,

Thea Devine

NIGHT MOVES
Thea Devine

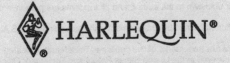

HARLEQUIN®

TORONTO • NEW YORK • LONDON
AMSTERDAM • PARIS • SYDNEY • HAMBURG
STOCKHOLM • ATHENS • TOKYO • MILAN • MADRID
PRAGUE • WARSAW • BUDAPEST • AUCKLAND

For my beloved John, who took me to Maine for the
first time all those years ago....

ISBN 0-373-25860-7

NIGHT MOVES

Copyright © 1999 by Thea Devine.

1

Truck McKelvey wouldn't have said that he had spent the last fifteen years dreaming about Carrie Spencer, but the day she blasted back into Paradise riding high and hard on her Harley, his hormones definitely stood up and took notice.

He watched from the front of Bob Verity's store as Carrie expertly swung the Harley in between his van and Bob's delivery truck, cut the engine and lifted off her helmet. She hadn't changed one bit. She still had that long streaked blond hair, still favored tight T-shirts under an oversize leather jacket and poured-into jeans.

And she still had those luscious red lips, and she was still concealing her beautiful blue eyes behind sunglasses. Fifteen years ago, she had been gorgeous, popular, a top student, sought after, elusive and driven.

And *his*. Once upon a time, she had almost given herself to him. Almost. He had been the only one to ever get that close. But Carrie Spencer had been determined she wasn't going to get stuck—not with a guy, a romance, a marriage or a baby. She was made and meant for bigger and better things and she was going to get them—alone.

And now here Carrie was, as aggressive and confrontational as ever, a regular warrior princess off to conquer the provincials on her trusty mechanical steed.

Truck didn't know if he was amazed, amused or just plain annoyed. One thing he did know was that Carrie

Spencer was a walking conflagration in which a man could be consumed if he got too close.

He'd watched heads turn as she roared down Main Street. They all saw the legs, the hair, the go-to-hell determination. And they all wanted her, instantly, the way he did. Just the sight of Carrie was arousing him, and he had no control over it whatsoever. Even after all these years and all this time, he was unbearably and unbelievably right-out-to-there aroused and he still had the inexplicable primitive urge to conquer her.

Goddamn...goddamn...maybe it was unfinished business. Maybe it was pride, but Truck wanted her still—against his will and against everything that made sense. And maybe, just maybe, he felt gratified by the way she was making a show of swinging her long legs over the seat because she knew he was watching her. He liked how her lips tightened and she lifted her chin as if she were going into battle. Maybe, Truck thought, it was war already.

There was no question Carrie knew exactly who he was. But she didn't hesitate as she stepped up onto the outdoor patio and around the spindly little tables and chairs set out for alfresco snacking. She tried to hide her dismay as she strode right up to where Truck stood with his arms crossed over his chest.

He was the last person she expected to see her first time back in town. Of *all* the people from her past to have to face right now. The one person, the one moment she wished she could erase forever.

It was true: your high school years were the ones closest to your heart; Carrie felt the pain and the past mingle together instantly. She felt seventeen again. Truck looked no different than he had looked fifteen years before: the long dark hair, the arresting features that had only improved with age, the tight jeans, the boots, the dark T-shirt, the direct dark gaze that made you feel feminine and sexy.

And *his*.

Truck could have been waiting there just for her. Maybe she had shot back in time and fate was giving her another chance to play the scene the way she had rerun it endlessly in her mind for months and months after it happened.

But no. Fate had been kind. Because she hadn't succumbed to the sexual magnetism of the young Truck McKelvey, she'd been able to move to New York and make something of herself. She'd had a great job in advertising, great friends, a great life that hadn't included bad boys and babies.

How much she had learned about herself since then. But Truck already knew too much about her, and his bold assessing gaze told her that his memories hadn't been fleeting either, and that the sight of her had raised them right up under his skin all over again.

It was time to confront the enemy on his turf. Carrie wasn't scared of him. Or the past. Or her lightning-bolt feelings.

She took off her sunglasses, and her bright-blue gaze skewered him. "Truck."

"Carrie," he said coolly.

"Still here, I see."

"So are you."

That was too pointed a comment for Carrie's comfort. "Small world," she murmured.

It hadn't taken thirty seconds. Truck felt like strangling her. She went past him into the store, and after a moment's hesitation, he turned to watch her through the screen door.

It was a huge old-fashioned convenience store, carrying everything from pizza to shampoo, newspapers, groceries, milk, juice, soda, beer and paperback novels. Carrie Spencer was picking up what looked like a month's worth of necessities in the grocery section: paper goods, ice, coffee, bottled water, soup, canned vegetables, batteries, bread, cold cuts...the kind of things she would buy if she meant to stay for a while.

"Carrie Spencer...!" Bob Verity came out from behind the counter. "How you doin'?"

She popped up from behind one of the shelf units with two packages of cookies in hand. *Who on earth was he...? Oh jeez—Bob Verity...thirty pounds heavier.*

"I'm okay, Bob. How about you?"

He took the cookies and placed them on the counter with the rest of her purchases. "Decent, decent. Stayin' long?"

"Need some R and R," she said brightly, adding a big jar of peanut butter and a box of crackers to her pile. "It's a jungle out there."

"Tell me about it. On vacation?"

"Kind of," she said carefully. Bob had always been the town gossip. If you wanted everyone to know something, you told Bob. She could already see he was salivating to spread the news of her return. "Got this week's local paper?"

"It's a Saturday, Carrie, I'm usually sold out by Friday noon. I might have a copy back here though." He ducked behind the counter to check.

"But summer residents couldn't all be up yet," Carrie commented, taking a quart of milk and a gallon jug of juice out of the refrigerated section.

"Well, a fair number have come by already to reserve their papers. And now you. It's been a long time."

"Yeah."

"Since your mom died."

"I know." Carrie added a block of butter, a loaf of bread. She would make toast tomorrow morning. A tingling little memory. *Her mother had always made her toast in the morning.* Now why had she remembered that? Don't go there, she warned herself. She didn't want to think about her mother. Or talk about her. Or how long it had been.

"Always thought you should've rented the place out."

"I didn't need to," she said, keeping her voice neutral.

"And now?"

"I'm on vacation. I think that's it for today anyway."

"Sure enough." Bob began adding up her purchases.

Truck was leaning against the wall when she emerged with three bags in each hand.

"Need some help?"

"You have to work for tips now?"

"At least I'm working. How about you?"

That got to her. It was as if everyone's radar was operating overtime. They could smell a tall tale a mile away. And she needed time to regroup and reconsider what her cover story was going to be.

"I'm on vacation. From that big city, big-time job. Remember? I know I sent the announcement to the paper. Anyway, I think we can achieve some equanimity here—I won't have to see you again, and you won't have to see me."

"I wouldn't count on it," he murmured.

"I am depending on it."

"Oh, I think you will be depending on me, Carrie."

"Not for anything I can think of in this lifetime," she

snapped as she shoved forty dollars' worth of groceries into her saddlebags.

"Maybe there'll be something you can think of this weekend," he suggested as she jammed her helmet down and revved the engine.

"Oh no, Truck McKelvey, the last thing I'll be thinking about this weekend is you," Carrie retorted. Then she pushed the cycle out from between the two trucks, jammed her foot down on the accelerator and disappeared in a cloud of dust.

"Feisty li'l thing, ain't she?" Bob commented from behind the screen door. "She ain't been down the Pond Road for years."

"I know."

"She's gonna die when she sees the house."

"Well, I kept the roof intact at least," Truck said. "I paid some kids to take off the snow every winter. I used to do it for her mother the year before she died. But that's about it. I couldn't vouch for the plumbing or the electricity. I hope she remembers she's got to turn things on."

"There's lots of things Carrie's got to remember," Bob said thoughtfully. "What d'you suppose the real story is?"

"You heard her—rest, relaxation, vacation."

"Paradise, Maine, instead of Paris, France? I don't think so."

"It works for me," Truck said, opening the screen door and moving inside. "Speaking of which, I'm still working. Got the lunch order? I'm going down to Portland this afternoon to spec out a new job. I'll just take mine. You can have Danny pick up the rest." Danny had worked with Truck over a year now and was shaping up to be a big help.

"Done and done," Bob said. "You gonna go and check on Carrie later?"

"Maybe," Truck said noncommittally. Bob could sniff out carnal interest at forty paces. After overhearing that exchange between him and Carrie, the storekeeper was going to be expecting updates at the very least.

Truck had to throw him off the scent fast. "I'm not the only one who lives up the Pond Road," he said pointedly.

"You're the closest. Besides, making sure Carrie settles in okay is the neighborly thing to do," Bob said.

"If you're so concerned, you go pay her a visit."

"Hell, I'd be useless. All I can bring her is popovers. I can't fix her plumbing. Plus, I'm married. Come on, Truck, aren't you curious at all about Carrie coming back to Paradise like this?"

"Nope," Truck said, shrugging. *Liar.* He tossed a five-dollar bill on the counter. "I'll see you tomorrow, probably," he added, heading out the door.

Or maybe not. Maybe Bob knew him too well, but Truck wasn't looking for trouble. He was perfectly content with the way things were, and Carrie Spencer living down the road shouldn't make a damn bit of difference in his life.

Like hell.

They'd hated each other growing up, he and Carrie. Just hated each other.

Carrie had been an expert in evasive maneuvers, who'd known exactly how to get every guy in school panting after her without giving away the store.

He'd had no interest at all in playing games, especially her kind of game. But in senior year, something had changed. He had changed. Or maybe she had. All it had taken was one glance—one sideswiping look of sex-

ual awareness between them. The sensation had been as
direct as a bullet and equally as devastating. The tension
between them had escalated day after day, week after
week, as they'd circled each other warily. Their first kiss
had been hot, wet, explosive. He'd wanted to live in her
mouth forever. They'd spent hours together, and he'd
learned her like a book. Every turn-on, every pleasure
point. His hands, his mouth, his body had become intimate with her on every level but one.

But Truck had waited. He had reined in his overwhelming need to possess her, understanding instinctively that the waiting would heighten their ultimate
joining into something out of this world. He'd felt as if
he were preparing all his life for that one shattering moment. And then, just when they'd been on the brink,
poised, pulsating and bursting with need, she'd
wrenched away from him, claiming she'd been using
him just the way he'd been using her, and had an-
nounced she didn't want him after all. Truck remembered all of it as if it were yesterday as he sped down
Route 1 toward Portland.

He had never felt like that about anyone, before or
since. And he didn't want to, ever again. It used up too
much energy. It was much easier to keep it casual and
then walk away with no ties, no emotional upsets, no
commitments. He had lived his life that way ever since
he'd returned to take over the business, and he would
have said he was a happy man. But he couldn't ignore
that lingering feeling of overwhelming desire for Carrie
that still lived on, after so many years.

Damn her. Damn her. Damn her.

He'd bet that Carrie's memories were damn selective
and that none of them included him. Suddenly he felt
the overpowering and irresistible male urge to heat

things up again and to make sure that this time she would never forget him.

NOTHING EVER CHANGED.

No, check that: things changed, but the basics didn't, like how you felt about things, places, people. Especially in small towns.

Carrie had forgotten about small towns. She had been feeling kind of nostalgic about Paradise after all this time. Big mistake.

Nothing ever changed here. It was one of its charms. On every visit home she'd made during her first years in New York, she had always been impressed by the sameness. Today, as she'd come into town, Carrie was struck once again by how Main Street looked exactly the same as it had when she'd been a child. Maybe she had always counted on that, she thought as she roared past the barbershop, the bank, the clothing store, the Main Street Furniture Shop, Longford's Hardware and the coffee shop.

Maybe everyone needed that kind of constancy in their lives. A town. A home, family, love.

No. She wasn't going to fall into that trap. She had never been a fan of hearth, home, family and small-town life. And she'd never been willing to give up anything.

All she had ever wanted or needed in Paradise was a weekend to refresh herself and the assurance that her mother was well and coping. Then she could dive back into the frenzy of work, much as she dived off the rocks into Freshwater Pond—with recklessness, audacity and a goal always in sight.

Carrie hadn't been back since her mother's death a year and a half before. Even then there had been little for her to do. Her mother had left everything wrapped up tidily, her only wish being that Carrie not sell the house, and keep coming home the way she always did. She'd chosen to close up the house instead.

And now she *was* coming home, but not at the top of her game as she'd always imagined. Instead, she was coming back out of work and out of options, with her motorcycle, and all that remained of her possessions crammed into a U-Drive rental truck parked at the Tree-tops Motel the next town over.

Presentation was everything, though. If Carrie had learned nothing else during her ten years in the cut-throat canyons of New York advertising, she'd learned that.

No one was going to see her sweat.

Still, it was all the same in the end, she thought as she paid her bill at the Treetops for one night's lodging with breakfast. Everyone came back eventually, especially when there was nowhere else to go.

She knew it better than anyone. There had been twenty candidates for every job she had applied for, and now with her high salary and ten years' experience, Carrie Spencer was a liability in a world where an assistant art director with five years under her belt could be hired for half the money Carrie required.

As she drove the van down Route 30 toward the house where she'd grown up, Carrie felt resentment clogging her throat like bile.

Get over it. It's done. It is what it is...

Carrie had no appreciation at all for the clear summer-blue sky over the tops of the trees that lined the Pond Road, nor any feeling of urgency when she glimpsed the glitter of water in the distance as she approached the turn to the house.

Almost there. Almost where? Where was she? And why did she suddenly feel lost?

Carrie shook off the sudden flare of apprehension as she turned onto the road down to the lake. It was really little more than a track, unpaved and overgrown. She jounced down a hundred yards of roots and dirt and maneuvered the van into the clearing where she'd always parked and jammed on the brake.

There, just ahead of her, on a rise above the lapping water, was the house, shuttered up, dilapidated and looking impossibly worn and weary.

Or maybe she was. *No.* She shook herself. She'd get nowhere thinking like that. She got out of the van, and just stood there, inhaling the scent of decaying wood, fresh summer growth and the unmistakable perfume of fresh air. She slowly walked toward the lake. She had always loved the lake. It had seemed vast to her when she was a child, as big as an ocean and as fathomless, its perimeter ringed by trees that hid the houses nearby. Then the solitude had felt peaceful. But today, as she stood on the rocks just below the house, she felt as if she was the only one here, and it felt lonely. Very lonely.

Hard as it was, Carrie had to come to terms with the undeniable fact that she was about to begin a new life...in an old place she'd believed she'd never, ever return to.

Now that she was here, she almost felt afraid to enter the house. *Mother...* A jolt of grief almost doubled her over. Her eyes blinded by tears, she turned to look at the house and began to walk toward it. It didn't look so desolate, except for the windows, which were shuttered up just like the past and all the years her mother had so quietly lived out her life on the Pond.

Don't think about that. She rummaged for her keys, and then stepped up onto the porch and unlocked the door.

Again, Carrie felt that unexpected reluctance to enter the house. She knew that everything would be exactly the way she remembered it. If she were blind, she could find her way around that small house because her mother had never changed anything.

Why? Why had everything remained the same all these years? Constancy? Certainty? She had never given it a moment's thought in her life and she didn't dare to think about it now.

Carrie pushed into the living room with its stone fireplace and huge wood stove, and stopped dead. She had known it would be cold inside but she had forgotten how musty and dank a closed-up, unlived-in house could be. It was eerie, even a little spooky, the contrast between the light and warmth outside, and the blackness and coldness within.

She should have called Jeannie Gerardo, her best friend from high school who lived right down the road so she wouldn't have had to face the darkness alone. Jeannie would have met her here, and made light of everything, even Carrie's momentary jitters. But it was too late for that since Jeannie was probably still at work.

This was something she'd have to face alone: an empty house. Memories of her mother. *Mother dying all alone...*

She shook off the feeling. Her mother had been the first one to encourage her to leave Paradise. Her mother had never held her back. Her mother had understood...

She propped the front door open and resolutely groped her way into the kitchen, and bumped right into the sharp edge of a counter.

She smothered a curse as she acclimated herself.

There was a small counter to the left of the door, the fridge was next to that, its door always banked open with a stool and the stove next to that. It was like being in a nightmare, touching sticky unidentifiable things in the dark, looking for the matches her mother always kept in the porcelain pot by the stove. She found canisters still filled with flour, tea bags and sugar. The coffee percolator her mother always stored in the bread box. The plastic container with the scouring pads. And then, just where it had always been, the matches in the pot by the stove. She struck one against the stone fireplace and the flame flared, instantly revealing the dusty furniture, cobwebs, must, mildew and decay.

Carrie felt her way to the electric box. One big plug fed every outlet. She shoved it into place and immediately all the lights flashed on.

Oh my God…

A mess. An unholy awful mess.

Mice and other creatures had taken over the house. There were tracks everywhere, right into the kitchen, and cobwebs and dust. Shredded newspaper and fabric. Worm-eaten wood by the fireplace.

There were dead things in the fridge and around the kitchen stove. The linoleum was tacky with some substance that had never been cleaned up. The bathroom was dusty, cobwebby, and the shower floor coated with who knows what.

Carrie almost couldn't bear to enter her mother's room. It was at the back of the house, tucked in the corner with views of the pond in the morning. Her mother had loved the view. She stepped into the room, and her eyes teared as she surveyed it. Everything made of cloth or wool had been eaten through and was spotted with tracks and recent moisture. Carrie took mental notes as she scrutinized the room. She'd have to do something about the mattress. She'd have to burn everything in the closet. Her hands shook as she backed out of the room, turned and headed for her bedroom.

There, only the down comforter was relatively untouched. She could drape it over the porch railing, beat it and air it out, and she would sleep on the sofa until she scrubbed and cleaned every surface in the house.

Every surface. She sank into the wooden desk chair in the little den next to her room, feeling overwhelmed and utterly daunted.

All this work before she could even get started remaking her own life.

There wasn't even a TV or radio. And she had sold all her possessions before she'd come north.

She supposed she was thankful the roof didn't leak. But she wasn't feeling thankful at all. She clenched her fists and squeezed back the tears.

It's done. I can't change it. I have to start from here and make it work... I have no choice... I have nothing.

No. No. *No!* That was really giving in to self-pity.

She did have something. She had a roof over her head and money enough for several months. And she had talent and determination. A lot of people had a lot less than that to work with when they had to start over.

All she had to do was take down some shutters and clean a house.

She would call Jeannie right now. She'd been planning to call Jeannie tomorrow, but Carrie needed a friend tonight.

It was only four in the afternoon, Carrie thought, not at all too early to renew a friendship and begin a new life.

2

JEANNIE GERADO LIVED a half mile down the Pond Road in the house her family had occupied since before Carrie was born. She was waiting at the door when Carrie arrived, and she didn't look a day older than when Carrie had left.

"Come to the kitchen and have some coffee," Jeannie said, and once again Carrie had the sensation of stepping back in time. The kitchen was exactly the same. The table, scrubbed and bare, was still surrounded by the same white-painted chairs, and the same ancient percolator was plugged into an outlet in the electric stove just as it had always been. The late-afternoon sun streamed in through the windows, which looked out onto the backyard.

Jeannie poured some coffee into a mug, handed it to Carrie, then joined her at the table. "You should have come sooner," she said, but she softened the words with a smile. She wore little makeup and no lipstick, and her best features were her wide mouth, shiny swinging brown hair and smiling brown eyes. Those eyes were looking at her with such compassion that Carrie felt a twinge of guilt.

"I should have," she agreed. "But I'm back now." She hadn't told Jeannie much on the phone, just that the house was a mess, her life was a mess, and she needed a friend. And she needed her mother, but it was years too late for that, and she pushed the thought away.

"For good?"

"For now."

"I don't believe it," Jeannie said firmly. "You couldn't stay away from New York for ten minutes—ever. I bet you already miss the money, the clothes, the men—"

"Things change."

"They sure do," Jeannie murmured. "There has to be a man."

"There always is," Carrie said.

"What's his name?"

Carrie lifted her cup to her lips. Therapy already; she hadn't been here ten minutes. But Jeannie was like that, sharp, sympathetic, discerning.

"Elliott. The weasel."

Jeannie waited.

Sighing, Carrie put down the mug. "I was fired," she said bluntly. "There isn't a job to be had at my level in this market. I can't get by on less unless I'm not in New York, so I'm not in New York."

"And this Elliott?"

"Corporate politics. Dirty, ugly politics, the upshot of which was he took away a client, my group was let go, and he was made a vice president." She took a sip of coffee to steady the tremor in her voice.

God, it still rankled. It had been months, and she still felt angry. She swallowed slowly to calm herself and went on, "Of course, I've always contended being made a vice president is the first step out the door. But that's probably pure envy on my part..."

"That's rotten," Jeannie said. That couldn't be the whole story, she thought. There had to be more. It was obvious from just the way Carrie said Elliott's name with such disgust. But it was too soon for that kind of confidence. The wound was too raw and recent.

"It was. But I'm dealing with it."

Jeannie was silent for a long moment. It was inconceivable to her that someone like Carrie who was so charismatic and talented couldn't have found work anywhere else in the country. Yet she also knew that people wanted to be where they wanted to be, and maybe Carrie wanted and needed to be here right now.

"I'm tired," Carrie said abruptly. "I really got tired. I was always on the run. Traveling. Doing the social scene. Pitching new ideas. Running to the client twenty times over after rewriting the same damn thing twenty times to change one word, one scene, one perspective. And then this last presentation..."

She got a faraway look in her eyes, as if she was picturing it, and Jeannie felt as if she could almost see it too.

"Elliott cut the show right out from under me," Carrie said, her voice harsh. "He was the big hero, I'll tell you. He *saved* the account, and gave credit where it was due to *his* brilliant concept and the hard work of *his* group. It was devastating. There was nothing I could do to stop him."

Carrie had done something, though. She'd come home for comfort. "That's just awful," Jeannie murmured. "You're here now. You did *something*. But I'm afraid you've traded all that glamour for church breakfasts, flea markets, biweekly town dances, local art shows and townies in trouble. Are you sure about this, Carrie?"

Carrie smiled wanly. "I'm not sure about anything except the mice are eating up my house, and Truck McKelvey's still in town."

"Oh yeah?" Jeannie slanted a glance at her.

"I saw him at Verity's store. And Bob!"

"Yep, Bob took over. Just like Truck. Truck came back from the Midwest about, oh, eight years ago, and took over the plumbing business from Old Man. Old Man...well, he's an old man, and—Truck's a damn good plumber."

"I bet," Carrie muttered.

Jeannie caught the tone in her voice and she perked up. "Not married," she added craftily. "Not engaged."

"But lots of friends, I bet," Carrie put in dryly.

"Everywhere," Jeannie said. "If he's seeing anyone, she doesn't live in Paradise. He's always at every social function."

"Oh sure. Even the dances?"

"Absolutely. He loves to dance. I wish Eddie did," Jeannie said wistfully. "He likes to watch, and not me." The bitterness was there even though she tried to hide it. Twelve years with Eddie, good-natured, friendly Eddie with the roving eye...but that wasn't Carrie's concern. Jeannie could handle Eddie. She'd been doing it all along.

She caught Carrie's questioning look and brushed it off. "Anyway, everyone comes and it's a lot of fun, and you'll come too next time. Oh, and there's a lake association now. You might want to join that."

"I never was an activist," Carrie warned her.

"But you are," Jeannie said. "Think of it this way— you've actively taken control of your life."

CARRIE DIDN'T FEEL at all in control when all hell broke loose the next morning.

She had forgotten to set the water heater; the kitchen faucet ran rust; the toilet water was brackish and backed up when she flushed; and when she tried the shower, the pipe burst and ice-cold water gushed all over her, and as she watched in horror it inched up slowly toward the edge of the shower stall.

Where was a plumber when you needed one?

They always called Old Man McKelvey, always. The number was right by the phone just as it had always been. It was ridiculous to hesitate to call him because Truck might answer.

She slogged out of the shower and reached for the phone and called Jeannie instead.

"I've got burst pipes and rising water," she told her, trying not to sound panicky.

"Call Truck. He'll fix it."

"I can't," Carrie hedged. "It looks worse than I think it is, and that will mean money I haven't got."

"Truck won't bite you, you know." Jeannie said. "You afraid of him or something? He's come and fixed my washing machine a dozen times and I'm still alive."

Carrie grimaced. She'd have to face him sometime, and she'd have to eat her words too. "I have some profit-sharing money coming. I'll call New York before I start having conferences with Truck." Only, the water was pooling at her feet now, and she had a feeling she didn't have that kind of time.

"Well, call Cain's over in Segers. Only everyone will wonder why you didn't call Truck."

"Fine. I'll call your golden boy after I speak to New York."

"Good," Jeannie said, laughing. "Now, why don't you plan to come to the dance Saturday night?"

"Is there one?" Carrie asked distractedly.

"Sure is. And you can meet some of the other golden boys in town."

"Which ones are they?"

"Oh, the ones who play doctor and lawyer. More to your taste than a plumber, perhaps," Jeannie said airily. "Call Truck, Carrie, before you drown."

"GOOD GOD, Carrie."

She dropped the phone and whirled. There was Truck in the doorway, a devil in denim with a mean-looking leather tool belt draped around his hips, as if Jeannie had conjured him up with her words.

"Go away."

"Need a plumber?"

"I don't need you." *Oops—unthinking words. Dangerous words.*

"Yes, you do."

She looked up sharply, too aware of how skimpily she was dressed, how drenched she was, how intensely he was looking at her, how inexorably the water was flowing around her feet and into the living room.

"I need a shutoff valve."

"Me too," he murmured. God, she was gorgeous. She was dressed in next-to-nothing shorts that elongated her legs up to there, and she was braless in the wet T-shirt that was molded to her breasts and nipples.

She might as well have been stark naked.

"Are you just going to stand there?" she demanded.

"Did you need a plumber, Carrie?" He kept his voice neutral with an effort. She had no business looking so impossibly sexy so early in the morning, and he had no business reacting to her as if he was seventeen and she was a pinup.

"*Would* you?" she asked with exaggerated politeness.

"Why don't you make some coffee?"

"Ah, yes—anything to distract the little woman."

His eyes swept over her, lingering on her breasts. He

remembered those breasts, how just one touch, one hot lick...he stiffened uncontrollably.

"There's nothing *little* about you, Carrie."

"Or you," she retorted.

"You need a man around the house," he murmured.

"I need a plumber, nothing more, nothing less," she ground out, and stamped into the kitchen. A moment later, the sound of pouring water ceased. She *didn't* need a man; she just needed to know those indefinable male *things* like where shutoff valves were and how to unstop toilets.

Using bottled water, she made the coffee in the ancient percolator.

She put milk, sugar and a package of cookies out on the counter and rummaged for clean cups and spoons.

Truck McKelvey was getting more than he deserved.

Carrie poured herself some coffee and went onto the porch. It was a sparkling clear morning with a crispness in the air that chilled her waterlogged body. She hunched down on the wobbly wicker chair, drew up her legs and balanced her cup on her knees. The pipes were clanking so loud she could hear them even from a distance. She just knew Truck was going to give her bad news. He wandered out shortly afterward with his coffee and nudged his hip onto the porch railing.

"Brought you some wood."

"Thanks." No smart-alecky retort about that. That was what neighbors did in Paradise: when you came to town with nothing, they brought you wood and wisdom.

"Pipes need redoing," he said matter-of-factly.

"Put 'em together with spit and duct tape," she said, shrugging.

"You're not going to be able to use the shower."

"So I'll bathe in the lake."

"Too cold yet," he said, eyeing her.

"You know every damn thing."

"I know that plumbing has to be redone, Carrie."

"I can't afford it," she said brusquely.

"How long are you staying?"

She lifted her head and met his dark lancing gaze directly. "Through the summer. I'll manage."

"You won't. Something else in the bathroom will go, or in the kitchen."

"I can't do it."

"Or you won't? The house isn't worth it, Carrie? Are you going away for fifteen more years?"

Oh, the house was worth it. It was a sturdy old house on a big lake in a picturesque Maine town, and it was her only asset right now. Truck didn't have to know that, she thought, and glanced over at him. She didn't like the way he was studying her.

"I can't afford it, Truck," she said quietly this time.

"Okay. I'll do it as side work. Afternoons, evenings, weekends. It won't cost you as much. And it'll add ten thousand to the price of the house."

"I wasn't planning to sell."

"Then you're going to stay?"

He'd painted her right into the corner, and he was watching her like the spider with a fly. She wasn't about to tell him she was out of a job, and that there was very little money. Not yet anyway. "You have an installment plan?" she asked lightly.

"It has to be done, Carrie."

She was beginning to think coming back to Paradise was a very bad idea.

"I can patch up the shower so you can use it today."

"I've already had a shower, thank you. Just make sure I can use it tomorrow."

"I'm doing the pipes, Carrie."

"Fine. Who am I to argue with you?" She unwrapped herself from the chair and eased to her feet. "I'll take your cup." She held out her hand. Truck touched her with his long strong fingers and his glimmering gaze, and she felt the shock clear through her body. Not possible. How could that kind of reaction be possible after all these years? She wasn't going to let it be possible.

"I have work to do," Carrie said abruptly, still conscious of her damp shirt and bare legs, and the magnetic pull of his dark knowing eyes lingering on her breasts... just *there*.

"I'll get the shutters down."

That was the last thing she expected him to say. She didn't want his help, his charity.

"Truck..." It was futile to even protest. He had a ladder up to the side of the house before she even said the words. So she went back inside and began mopping up the wet floor in the hallway and bathroom.

Truck finished removing the shutters and began stacking the wood he'd brought to one side of the porch. When she'd gotten the floor as dry as she could, she tackled the kitchen counters while he brought in the suitcases, boxes and art supplies that were still in her van. Next she stripped the beds and vacuumed the bedrooms, as Truck unpacked her computer and set it up in the den. They did all this in a calm companionable silence that simmered just below the surface with a kinetic tension.

It felt scary.

Carrie was scared to death seeing him moving around in her bedroom. Then suddenly he was standing on the threshold, as if he was waiting for her. Instantly the air became charged with heat, awareness, desire. She stood rooted to the spot for one long minute, caught by the brooding look in his eyes. This was insanity. She wasn't seventeen, even if she was experiencing some of those old emotions. It was just that Truck was too potent, and she was too vulnerable. She moved first, stepping backward. He followed, matching her step for step.

"Everything works, Carrie."

She couldn't resist looking him up and down as she veered pointedly toward the front door. "I can tell."

"I'll start work tomorrow."

"I think you've started already," she said tartly.

"I never start anything I can't finish. A hard lesson I learned in my youth."

Carrie didn't move an inch. She ignored all the bells going off in her head. She ignored everything except the pulsating heat of him inches away from her. She could melt under all that heat. "You must have a job somewhere to go to."

"I appreciate your concern, but plumbers make real good money, even in Paradise."

"Must be heaven," she murmured, opening the door wider.

Truck looked at her consideringly for a long moment, as if he was waiting for something, wanting something. Something she was not going to give him.

"Maybe," he said, "just maybe we make our own heaven." Then he moved away from her and out to his van, and without a backward look he left her.

IT WAS NO LONGER a house of horrors.

After her visit with Jeannie, Carrie had driven back to town for cleaning supplies, trash bags, the longest pair of barbecue tongs she could find, sheets, pillows, vacuum-cleaner bags, and a radio. Then she had forced herself to take the tongs and systematically pick up all the ugly icky things. The shapeless shredded things. The things she didn't want to know what they were. She filled two trash bags and lugged them up to the battered garbage cans by the road, feeling as if she had won the war. Only after that had she been able to sleep, curled on the couch in the aired-out comforter, lulled by a soothing voice on the radio and the twittery night sounds of the country.

If there had been no shower disaster this morning, she would have felt perfectly content sitting on the porch and having her second cup of coffee as she read the local newspaper. There had been a shower disaster, though, and Truck had shown up like some knight errant. Of course, he had been looking after the place since her mother had died, and knew the state the plumbing was in. It didn't take psychic powers to figure out what was likely to happen when she tried out the shower. So Truck had come to help out. So what? So why was she so surprised...and unsettled by his appearance?

I think you will be depending on me, Carrie. Maybe there'll be something you can think of this weekend...

Still, he was too damn cocky for his own good. It didn't matter. Carrie was not going to let him trade on the past. Anyway, they had no past, and she was going to make very sure they had no present.

Carrie knew what she had to do. She had to send out a thousand résumés, and network like crazy, on-line and by fax, phone every contact, follow up every lead, and answer every ad until she found a job.

One focus. No distractions.

If Truck wanted to provide the hot and cold running

water, fine. It didn't entitle him to hot and cold running commentary as well.

"So?" Bob looked inquiringly at him across the counter.

"What?"

"How bad was it?"

"How bad was what?"

"Take your pick. The house or Carrie's temper."

"Right out of a Stephen King novel. Lots of creepy-crawly things. And bad pipes. Does that satisfy your evil curiosity? You got Old Man's paper?"

Bob handed it across the counter. "So, are you gonna do some work on the house?"

"Might."

"You're pretty closemouthed, pal."

"Nothing to tell, Bob, I spent the day in Portland."

"Didja?"

"Yup."

"Carrie went to Portland."

"Did she?" Truck said in a disinterested tone as he scanned the paper. He knew that; he'd seen her zoom by. "How do you know that?"

"She came through town on the bike about a half hour ago. So it figures she brought the van back. Only place is Portland. Maybe you saw her there?"

"You're a regular Sherlock Holmes." He tosssed a dollar on the counter. "See you."

It seemed that he couldn't avoid talking about Carrie. When he got home, even Old Man, ensconced in his wheelchair by the picture window in the living room, put in his two cents, the minute Truck came through the door.

"So how is she?" his father asked.

"Strong. Prickly."

"Hasn't changed a bit," Old Man said.

His memory was sharp as a tack, nothing escaped him.

"The house was a disaster area."

"How bad?"

"About what you'd think after being vacant for a year and a half."

"So you'll do what needs to be done," Old Man said.

"Guess I will," Truck said. Neighbor helping neighbor. It was the only way.

"Get Danny down to Portland, if you have to."

Truck had already decided the young man had proved his merit, but he only nodded as he washed up at the kitchen sink. "How you doing today?"

"Tolerable," Old Man said. "Jolley came and cleaned today. Mail's on the table."

The housekeeper always came twice a week, and on those days the house felt most like a real home, or at least how Truck imagined a home to be. The dinner was always in the oven, the table nicely set and Old Man was waiting for him, to hear how his day went and tell Truck how his day had gone. This ritual was comforting to both of them.

His father always had something to do. Truck had moved company operations to the house and built an office onto the back where Old Man worked the computer, estimating jobs, making appointments and preparing the bills.

It gave Old Man's life manageable parameters and a sense of purpose after the terrible tragedy of the trucking accident that had left him paralyzed from the waist down.

He was still part of the company even though he had handed it over to Truck, and every night over dinner,

Truck made sure they discussed the business of the day. Each evening at exactly eight o'clock he helped Old Man to bed, and if he were going out, he alerted the emergency service to monitor the house. Old Man never asked questions. And Truck didn't always go out. Some nights it wasn't worth it.

Especially since Carrie had come back, and he was dog-tired from spending the night tossing and turning, tormented by his vivid dreams about Carrie Spencer. Carrie and those legs. Carrie and that T-shirt. He could almost taste the texture of her skin. Could almost feel her body moving under his hands.

She'd given all that up to go out and conquer the world. Now she was back, she had issued a challenge no man could resist, and he swore this time he was going to conquer her.

And tomorrow wasn't too soon to begin.

3

"SO, TRUCK'S GOING to do the plumbing," Jeannie murmured as she sat across from Carrie that evening and watched her shuffle papers. She had come over to check up on Carrie, and to make sure that she'd done something about the pipes. And she'd come for company, though she didn't want to admit it.

"Guess so. He was pretty insistent about it."

"That's my Trucker," Jeannie said fondly. "So now what?"

"What do you mean, now what?"

"I mean..." Jeannie's eyes gleamed. "What about Truck?"

"He's lethal, and you know our history. How can you ask that?"

"Just...wondering."

"Don't get any ideas," Carrie said. "You have a look in your eye I distinctly don't like. Which reminds me of why I don't like small towns. Everybody knows your business. And everybody meddles."

"But there's nothing to meddle in," Jeannie said. "Or is there?"

"If you think you're going to set something up, Jeannie, forget it. I'm here to rest, regroup and look for a job. When I find one, I'm out of here."

"Ummm," Jeannie murmured, staring at her coffee. "Still have that aversion to marriage and mommyhood."

"Motherhood does not appeal to me. I am not going to be trapped. Look at my mom. She's the sole reason I never got into trouble..."

"Whereas you probably got into plenty of trouble once you got to New York."

"That's *my* business, Jeannie," Carrie said, lightly but firmly. She had absolutely no desire to talk about those years of futile, dead-end relationships built on the shifting sands of office politics and cute meets in the local hangouts. Yes, she'd thought she'd been in love, more than once, but those connections had all petered out because she'd been so focused on building her career. You couldn't sustain anything when you were that consumed with being a success; you burned out before you even could think about building a life.

"But my Mom was *stuck* here," she added, "and I swore I would never be at the mercy of my hormones or any man."

"Maybe I'm too romantic for my own good," Jeannie said, "but I do believe you're going to tumble someday and get caught in an avalanche."

"Oh, nonsense."

"You protest too much. There are some really neat guys who've settled in town. The chamber of commerce made a concerted effort to draw young professionals from Portland. Advertised the quality of life an hour away, that sort of thing. I wasn't kidding about the golden boys." Jeannie watched Carrie's face, "Okay, Truck's lived here all his life, but Peter Stoddard, Dr. Tom Kelsey, Dan Durand, they're all new in town and as eligible as anyone you'll find at a singles' bar in New York."

Carrie wrinkled her nose in distaste. "Please..."

"You are coming to the dance on Saturday night?"

"Oh, the dance," Carrie said faintly. She had almost forgotten about the dance.

"At the Grange Hall," Jeannie prompted. "With all those guys I've been telling you about."

"You sure are determined to thrust me into the social whirl, and way before I'm ready," Carrie said. "Fine. I'm coming."

"Of course you are," Jeannie said. "So now we come to the real reason I came over tonight. We can choose something for you to wear."

Jeannie followed Carrie to her old bedroom. A mountain of clothes was piled on the bed and crowded into the armoire, and accessories to match were scattered haphazardly on the dresser and the floor.

"Oh my God," Jeannie breathed, stroking a suede skirt that felt like butter. "Oh my. This is just luscious. Oh, Carrie..."

"Rummage to your heart's content," Carrie urged. "Do you get very dressed up for these events?"

"We don't wear evening gowns," Jeannie said, holding a long lean black dress up in front of her. "Size—what?—did you say?"

"Ten. And I was thinking more along these lines." Carrie pulled out a denim jumper that she usually wore on the weekends.

Jeannie shook her head. "Nobody'll ever see your lines in that."

"I'm looking to draw some lines, Jeannie. I don't need attention."

"Everyone needs attention," Jeannie said, her tone sharper than she had intended. She held up her hand. "Forget I said that." Jeanne then began to go through the piles on the bed and selected a dress. "Here, wear this."

It was an outfit Carrie had often worn to the office,

one-piece cut to look like a tunic and skirt in a soft shade of blue.

"I will. That's one of my favorite dresses, by the way."

"It's beautiful." There was no envy in Jeannie's voice, just an undercurrent of longing to be able to afford something like that.

Jeannie had never had the drive and determination to go any farther than Paradise. She'd been content to marry Eddie after two years of dates and breakups and reconciliations, and she'd been working in the local bank since. She'd graduated from high school. If it weren't for those stinging little remarks Jeannie kept making, Carrie would have thought her friend had no regrets at all.

"Well, all right," Jeannie said as she prepared to leave. "That's settled. Are you going to drive or do you need a lift?"

"I'll drive. I think I can find the Grange Hall. I don't want to pick up any fast rides home. I know these country boys."

"Oh, I'm not sure you do," Jeannie said. "I'm not sure *I* do. The dance starts at eight."

"I'll be there."

"Make sure. Bob's passed the word by now. There might even be an announcement in the paper."

"You're kidding."

"Hey—Pat Boucker, who lives over the other side of the town road—she writes the Paradise local news column for the Segers paper. It'll be in there. In fact, if Truck does your plumbing, she'll probably report it."

"Jeannie," Carrie said warningly.

"Honest. Everything's fair game." Jeannie scooted out the door. "Wait till you see."

"I don't want to see," Carrie said.

"Oh, come on, you're just not used to people *caring* about you."

"Is that what you call it?"

"Yeah," Jeannie said softly. "That's what I call it. It's a damn sight nicer than being completely anonymous and...alone. I don't know how anyone can live that way. That's why I'm here and you went there."

"Well, I'm here now, I guess I'll get used to it," Carrie said philosophically. But she wasn't sure she ever would, she thought as she closed the door behind Jeannie. She hadn't been home one day, and she was already beginning to feel trapped.

THE NEXT MORNING Carrie felt frenzied. It always happened when she was in Paradise, and Jeannie's visit last night had not helped.

It had just reminded her again of what she didn't like about small-town life, like having to travel more than three minutes to get anywhere. And she didn't like the silence of the woods or how time stretched out in a way that made it seem interminable. And most of all, she didn't like Truck McKelvey invading her space. He was coming. This afternoon he was coming, and she was feeling frenzied about that, too.

She had spent the morning on a job search. The living-room table was scattered with papers, résumés, envelopes and stamps. The light poured in the front window. She had a rock station playing low on the radio, a cup of coffee by her hand, and she felt clean, comfortable, cozy and safe.

Safe now. But she didn't like how much time she'd spent debating what she would wear today before she settled on black jeans and a cream silk shirt.

Okay. Truck would come. He would do his thing with

the pipes, then the bill would arrive and she would pay it somehow and this business with the pipes—and Truck—would be over, done, finished.

It sounded perfectly normal, like the chores she'd done yesterday after she'd returned the van; she'd shopped for groceries, put away clothes and cleaned the house one more time again.

For herself. *Not* for Truck McKelvey.

Last night, after switching the mattress with the one in her old room, she had slept in her mother's bed and awakened to a lush view of woods and water, the sparkle of the sun on lapping waves.

This morning, she'd had her breakfast at the kitchen counter, and watched boats skimming across the lake.

Then she had gotten down to business. She'd wired the phone into the den and into her computer, gotten a new access number, and she had spent the morning answering E-mail and printing out job postings.

She'd showered in spite of the sputtering pipes, and now it was all of two o'clock and she was feeling jittery because the afternoon was young and she had nowhere to go and nothing urgent to do.

In her old life, she would probably have still been out to lunch with a client, in strategy meetings or racing around to put the finishing touches on a presentation. God, she missed it. She missed the rush of meeting problems head-on and solving them, and the pulse and beat of a business environment. She missed her colleagues, her friends, the little neighborhood restaurants, the germination of an idea on a napkin over a drink after dinner.

She didn't know what she was going to do with herself in Paradise. Jeannie was right. She really couldn't be away from the city for more than ten minutes. Or two days.

She was going to have to learn to cook. No more quick dashes down the block for a last-minute dinner-to-go at the salad bar. She was going to have to plan ahead. No more racing back and forth to do Saturday chores. She'd have to remember to group everything together in the same direction when she was going to town. She was going to have to clean the house once a week. Dear God, she was going to have to revamp her whole life.

What if she wound up staying in Paradise, and working from home? Winters in Maine with the snow up to the windows and the lake a sheet of sheer ice and power lines down? She'd be ready for the asylum. She *had* to be out of there by then.

Restlessly, Carrie moved to the table. While she was in the midst of sorting through the papers piled there, she heard the unmistakable hum of an engine in the distance. Going over to the window she saw Truck pull the van into the clearing, jump out and stride purposefully toward the house. Lord, he looked good. Too good. He was wearing jeans and a black sleeveless T-shirt, and he was lean and tall, and his hair was black as a crow's wing in the sun. He looked young, sexy, potent. Her breath caught, and as she wheeled away from the window she almost collided with him. Truck reached out to steady her, and she felt his hands, his large capable clever hands, burning her skin through her silk-sleeved arms.

"Thanks. Hi."

"Hi, yourself." He was mesmerized by the sight of Carrie. Silk the color of whipped vanilla was draped over her upper torso and buttoned up to the enticing vee between her breasts. No jewelry. No makeup. Her hair tumbling from an untidy topknot. Her lower lip moist and tender, as if she had been licking it. She was as sexy as hell. A man had to have a will of iron to remove his hands from her.

"So—you're...ready to start," Carrie said and there was a curious tension in her voice.

"I'm ready to start," Truck said, very reluctantly relinquishing his grip. "I just have to get underneath."

"Not a lot of wiggle room down there," she teased.

"Oh, I'll get in," he murmured. "I'm familiar with it."

"How nice you're such an expert."

"I just knew you'd appreciate that."

"I do. I like a man who's good with his hands." Oh, Lord, why had she said that?

She was being too coy by half. What the hell did she think she was doing?

"We don't have to play games, Carrie."

Oh, there was a note in his voice that made her very wary.

"I don't play games."

He sent her a skeptical look. Her expression was guarded, the warrior princess girding for battle because she had already given too much to the enemy. He wanted to breach her defenses and make her cry for mercy. Some knight he was. All he had to win her was a lock wrench for a lance and copper pipe for a sword, and they were damn puny weapons against the powerful memories of the past. There were other subtler ways to captivate a warrior princess and he had time on his side. He could spend a year repairing her plumbing. He savored the thought.

"I don't play games either, Carrie. So shall I stay or go?"

He'd thrown the gauntlet just to see what she would

do. Carrie knew she was asking for trouble no matter what she said.

"I'm paying you to do a job," she said coolly.

"Exactly." He got it. "I'm going to work on the showerhead today, maybe insert a new riser. Want to watch?"

Carrie knew when she was licked. She didn't like that wicked gleam in his eyes. It really was time to retreat, if she were serious, if she wasn't going to let Truck get to her.

She was never going to admit he already had.

THE METALLIC SOUND of the clanking pipes finally drove her out of the house, as well as the heat in the little den where she was working. It was busy work anyway. Carrie didn't try to convince herself otherwise, or deny that the attraction of sitting in that suffocating little room was mainly that she knew Truck was so close by.

He was installing the pipes bottom to top, and it couldn't be easy working with his arms extended and all the piping above him. Nor was there much room beneath the house, maybe three or four feet. And it must be hotter than an oven down there.

She shook herself. It was crazy to have sympathy for him. She needed to change her clothes, which were sticking to her, and concentrate on getting a job...getting a life.

After donning a tank top and shorts, she wandered out onto the porch. It wasn't much cooler there, nor was there any breeze coming off the pond. Nevertheless, she made her way down to the water's edge and levered herself onto one of two flat rocks that had been set on either side of the path specifically for dangling feet in the low lapping water.

Carrie...don't go near the water...

Carrie...a storm's about to blow...
Stay close, Carrie. Don't go far.

She could hear her mother's voice as plain as day, carrying across the pond a clear three miles away to the edge of the boys' summer camp.

What's the profit in talking to those boys, Carrie? They're here six weeks and gone, and you'll never see them again.

The very risk had been the whole point, and the very act of sneaking into the camp to talk to those exotic creatures. She had lived for the summers when the boys came. They had brought with them the heady scent of the world from away and lives vastly different than the one she knew.

Then one summer the camp had closed down, so the shorefront remained exactly as it always had been: a clean white sanded beach guarded by a row of yawning boathouses.

"They recently rented the camp to a production company that was looking for a pristine location to film a teen scream flick," Truck said behind her. "You know the kind of thing—horror island summer camp. They made about twenty years' worth of profit just on that deal."

Carrie sighed. *Small towns. Everybody knows everything, even the bottom line. How was she going to do this coming from a place where no one knew anybody's business?*

Keep it neutral.

She shaded her eyes as she turned to look at him. He'd removed his T-shirt, and his torso was slick with perspiration and grease. It was the body of a man, muscular, defined, rough with hair—and she felt as though she had tumbled back back fifteen years because it was also the body of the boy she had known. She averted her eyes as he slipped down opposite her and began shucking his boots and socks. "It's like a blast furnace under that house. I won't even talk about the webs and the bugs..." He slanted a look at her as he dragged his feet in the water. "No sympathy, huh?"

"I can't afford it on top of the price of the plumbing."

Carrie caught his rueful smile out of the corner of her eye, that self-deprecating smile that turned a woman's knees to jelly and aroused every nurturing instinct. Even she wasn't immune to it, but that didn't mean she would just melt at the sight of it. Far from it—she was a woman with purpose and she wasn't going to let anything distract her.

She barely noticed that he had eased himself into the water and was walking out to a depth into which he could dive. He was treading water now, and washing his upper torso with a small cake of soap he had extracted from his jeans pocket. She was transfixed by the utterly male movement of his hands gliding over his arms, his chest, his belly...*Dear God, lead me not into temptation—it would be so easy...too easy...* Then he immersed himself to rinse off and dived in once again to swim vigorously back to shore.

He emerged like some primal god, glistening in the sun as the water poured off him, and he came slowly toward her, his sodden jeans clinging to his hips. It was a moment when a woman could fall in love. There was nothing like the boyish sight of a man drenched to the core and barely able to keep his pants on wading through the water to bow at her feet.

Carrie bit her lip. It couldn't be deliberate, she thought. They'd all swum in the pond since they could walk. It had to be this man, this day, and their history. He was as appealing as a seventeen-year-old and a hundred times more formidable as he stood there looking up at her, his hands planted on those narrow male hips. *Oh, Lord, those hips...*

Truck was too beguiling, too hot, and he was watching her too carefully. That intense awareness was there, sparking across the water, lifting her toward him to a place where she could crash and burn. It was time to end this. She couldn't afford to be sidetracked. Carrie scrambled to her feet. "Need a hand?"

Again that smile, that *knowing* devastating smile. "I'll take what I can get," he murmured, grasping her outstretched fingers and levering himself up onto the path.

Truck grabbed his boots and shoved his feet into them, then followed her up the path, admiring her long legs, the movement of her bottom in what were a pair of very conservative shorts, the tumble of her hair coming loose from her topknot, and her very no-nonsense attitude.

"There's soda, lemonade and tea in the fridge," Carrie said as they came up on the porch. "Help yourself."

Truck returned with two tall frosty glasses of lemonade and handed her one, and then nudged his hip against the railing, angling his body so he could look out over the pond.

"I could put in the dock if you want," he said.

"The wood's all rotten. I'm going to have to replace it, I guess someday. It's not a high priority right now," Carrie said.

"And you can always launch from Jeannie's dock if you want. Or mine."

"Right." Neighbors. Always there, always lending that helping hand. Carrie felt uncomfortable, as if even this offer came with strings. Or maybe it was just that Truck was offering, and it was too much already that he was working in her house at a *neighborly* consideration of her finances.

"So what's the real story, Carrie?"

She cringed. She had expected the question, though maybe not this soon, but it had been in the air from the moment she said she couldn't afford the repairs. She couldn't look at him. She didn't want to tell him, especially after that moment of connection at the pond. It would be so much easier to spin a juicy little lie and retain that high-powered image. Since there was nothing to say she wouldn't be in Paradise for the next ten years, let alone the next ten weeks, it was time to stop hiding.

She swallowed the lump in her throat along with the last gulp of lemonade. "I lost an account and I lost my job." She said it slowly and deliberately, as much to hear herself say the words—again—as to give him the explanation.

It still felt unreal as if she were on vacation and there was a definite end to this exile from her professional life. After all didn't she still have the fantasy that someone from the agency would call and say it had all been a mistake, that Elliott had confessed to his chicanery and given her the credit for the...?

"Tough," Truck said, pinning her with a dark unfathomable gaze.

Carrie pulled herself out of her reverie. "Brutal."

"So there's really no money."

"A severance package and some profit-sharing. My motorcycle and the clothes on my back," she said succinctly, as if enumerating her minuscule assets would reinforce the reality.

"And the house," Truck said gently. "You do have the house."

"And the house," Carrie agreed.

"And your friends," he added, noting the defiant spark in her eyes as he said it. He'd deliberately goaded her. Carrie hated any inference that she couldn't fend for herself. She had always been a fiercely independent girl who had never depended on anyone, and now she was a woman who had to depend on everyone.

Especially him. Truck found he liked that thought—a lot. It meant he had a chance; she wasn't going anywhere—yet.

"And my friends," she repeated softly.

"That's the way it is in Paradise," he murmured, setting aside his glass and reaching for his T-shirt. "I left my stuff under the house." He wrapped the shirt around his neck. "Finished?" He took her glass and his back into the kitchen.

Carrie jumped up and followed him, then wished she hadn't. In the small square kitchen, he loomed like danger, his bare chest radiating heat, his gaze glimmering with something she did not want to define. This was crazy. She didn't know why she hadn't stayed on the porch. It wasn't as if he didn't know where to put the glasses. He'd set them right in the sink and even put the lemonade pitcher in the fridge. A man who knew his way around the kitchen. She should like that. She just didn't want it to be *her* kitchen, *her* space. She wanted to tell him unequivocally to leave. *Now.*

The air thickened. The space was so small. She found herself backed against the hard edge of the counter with nowhere to move. And Truck knew it. There was this light in his eyes that made her want to chew pineboard. Truck knew exactly what he was doing and how he was doing it, and he was enjoying every moment of her vexation.

"I guess I'll see you soon," he said, making no move to leave.

"Soon...?" she echoed, her voice sounding suffocated.

"The dance."

"Oh." Right, she should have her head examined for promising Jeannie she'd come. "Yes, I'll be there."

"I know." Gorgeous independent Carrie Spencer doing the Texas twine down the center of the Grange Hall—it was a sight he couldn't wait to see. Not that she looked as if she was raring to go. Rather, she looked as if she expected him to kiss her. Truck relished the thought as he watched her squirm. She knew exactly what he was thinking.

Carrie wanted everything and she wanted nothing. Especially from him. Except maybe a kiss. Maybe...a soft touch of his lips. Maybe...the feeling of his skin touching hers. Maybe...a deeper thrust, a subtle invitation—it was in her eyes, in her provocative antagonistic stance.

Carrie was wearing the most sexless short and tank set, she smelled of a light teasing lemon scent, and she looked as desirable as hell. She looked as though she would take whatever he gave her and swear that she hated it. A man couldn't resist challenge like that. Not with a woman whose kisses were a burning memory in his soul.

He moved in on her then, slowly, slowly, slowly, letting the tension simmer as he deliberately fit his chest against her breasts and his hips against hers.

Carrie swallowed the sound she made at the back of her throat at the feel of his erection pressing against her. At that moment, more than life, Carrie wanted his kiss. Not because she wanted Truck; no, she wanted to prove to herself she needed no one.

She tilted her head. He slanted his mouth over hers.

"Still time to say no," Truck whispered, faintly amused that she was girding for battle. This was most definitely war, with the spoils nothing less than the admission that Carrie wanted him.

He'd seen the look in her eyes. Carrie was not immune to the old feelings. "Hold still," he murmured, cupping her chin, and ever so gently, he settled his mouth on hers. Just like that. Just the softest pressure, the longest sigh.

Her body twinged. Carrie felt the sensation spiraling downward, helplessly, between her legs. *No...yes—I don't care...*

He flicked her lips with his tongue, and she slowly opened her mouth to him. Slowly he entered, savoring the feel of her, the taste of her, the rhythm of her kiss. Devastating. He could barely keep himself in check. What was his problem? He wasn't a hormonally hysterical teenager anymore. Then why did he feel like one? And that he'd finally come home?

"Carrie...?" Barely above a breath, his lips hovering just above hers. "Tell me what you want."

She moistened her throbbing lips. His glimmering gaze followed every movement. "I want you to go away."

He followed the line of her tongue with his own. "Which way, Carrie? This way?" He pushed tighter against the cradle of her hips. "Or this way?" He slipped his tongue between her lips, sneaking behind her defenses once again.

She caved against him. How did you fight such provocative kisses? Why did she want to? But she knew: because she would be leaving. Someday soon, she would go, so why start any kind of relationship with Truck? She'd only have to leave him behind.

Right. Time for a reality check. "Truck..."

"Right here."

"Um, I understand this kind of thing could be seen to have some peripheral relationship to plumbing, but—"

"Only if you don't talk." He delved into her mouth again.

Carrie wriggled against him, terribly aware of all that muscle and sinew, and the fact she was making things worse. How had she gotten into this situation? "I think it's safer to talk."

"Maybe not safer."

Men had all the answers. "All right. Safer if you go."

"Safe for—whom, did you say?" he murmured, sliding his hands gently up and down her midriff.

Dear Lord, he remembered. Of all the things for him to remember, Carrie thought frantically. It begged the question what else he remembered. She could think of a dozen things, a dozen secrets she thought had been buried long ago.

This was a major error in judgment. And his face was so close to hers, and his mouth, and those glinting eyes. His warmth. His scent. All the things she remembered that made him so seductive and tantalizing...when she was seventeen. *Who was the adult here?* she wondered fuzzily. *Me.*

"Me," she said out loud, maybe just a little testily. "And better for you."

"Better for now maybe," he said lightly. "Maybe."

"Too many maybes," Carrie said. "I don't do maybes."

Truck looked at her for a long moment, then he removed his hands. Carrie was in warrior-princess mode, feeling too much and too vulnerable, and prickly as a porcupine, to boot.

Well, he was a man who knew how to wait. He'd waited fifteen years. He moved away from her and into the living room. Safe neutral territory there.

"Okay," he said, untying his shirt and slipping it on. That was safe too, even though he was keenly aware that Carrie watched his every movement. She couldn't help herself any more than he; there was a highly charged link between them, and it didn't have much to do with two fumbling teenagers. If Carrie needed to feel safe, he'd make her feel safe as a fortress, so be it.

"Tell you what," he said. "Let's do Saturday instead."

Carrie blinked. "What?" She bit her lip. What was she doing, chasing him away and then avidly watching his hands. Oh, those hands, those wicked, tempting hands. *What* had he said? Do Saturday?

"Sure," she said, still bemused. "Maybe."

4

MAYBE?

Maybe not.

She had to be crazy, Carrie thought. Truck McKelvey was not on her schedule of things to take care of this summer. She could not allow *that* man anywhere near her or her kitchen ever again. He was too steamy, too alluring, too all-fired *there*.

Who would have guessed? Fifteen years had passed, and the effect Truck had on her was just as potent as ever. All she had to do was look at him and her temperature soared just as it had that year that she had let him get so close. Too close. Close enough she'd almost gotten burned, she'd wanted him that bad. But not bad enough to give up her dreams. And she'd been right. She'd been a success, had gotten most of what she'd wanted. She'd had a fabulous career, a high-flying lifestyle, money and men, and no one to whom she had ever wanted to make a committment. And she'd liked it that way. Until Elliott.

Her stomach churned just thinking about him. The wonder boy. The creative genius who had set the benchmark for cutting-edge advertising. Elliott had forged a name for himself in the arena of memorable and quirky ad campaigns, and if some of them didn't quite increase the projected market share, well, Elliott always had a theory and an excuse and another agency hungry to pay him big money for his ideas.

Global Vision International had been the fifth agency to employ him in four years.

He had been assigned to Carrie's team and to one of her top clients, who was looking for a fast way to update a very stodgy image and a product that was losing chunks of market share by the minute. Carrie couldn't bear to think about the rest. He'd stolen her ideas, and stolen her client, and in the end, Carrie had paid dearly for his lies and her gullibility. Worse even, she had fallen in love with him. They were the dream team who were going to turn the industry upside down.

Instead Elliott had turned her inside out, broken her heart and walked away to more accolades, a promotion and a still higher salary, and a profile in both the Sunday *New York Times* magazine and *Advertising Age* on how *he* had resuscitated a dying brand name.

Carrie felt as if he'd cut her to little pieces. She had thought she was experienced enough to deal with him. But she hadn't been. He'd used her and abandoned her, and the fact that she should have known, she should have seen it coming, made Elliot's massive betrayal even more humiliating and painful.

She felt as if she'd barely made it out of New York alive, and even then it had taken her three months with her landlord chomping for the high-priced rent she could no longer afford to pay to make the decision to return to Paradise.

Paradise. You walk in the door and all your past sins come back to haunt you.

And Truck McKelvey was one delicious sin, a forbidden temptation, and she wasn't going to get within a hundred yards of him again if she could help it.

So the wisest thing for her to do was not to go to the dance. Then she wouldn't see Truck, wouldn't put herself in the position of having to dance with him, wouldn't have to deal with him at all until he came back to finish up at the house.

That was sensible. Sane.

She called Jeannie and told her. Later that afternoon, as Carrie was collating yet another set of résumés on the kitchen counter, Jeannie turned up at her door.

"What are you doing here?" Carrie asked as she admitted her friend and waved her into the kitchen. "I know I told you I wasn't going to the dance tonight, so really you didn't have to come."

"Sure I did," Jeannie said, hopping onto a stool. "What's this? Your résumé?" She picked up the three pages and started reading. "Oh my goodness. Carrie! I had no idea..."

"Well, all that experience isn't worth much now, is it?" Carrie murmured as she braced her hip against the opposite stool and continued putting the pages together. "I've spent all this time E-mailing, faxing and sending out a hundred of these things with no response. And I'd already gone through the mill with the headhunters before I even left New York. I don't even know why I'm punishing myself by doing this."

"But—you worked on the *Sexy Lady* account..."

"I did. But that's a part of my long-buried past..."

"I love that perfume! Not that it's done me any good..."

Carrie looked up at her sharply. Another pinprick comment that seemed to indicate things weren't so good between Jeannie and her husband.

"Anyway," Jeannie went on, "the point is, tell me again why you aren't going tonight?"

"I changed my mind."

"Oh." Jeannie recognized that tone.

Carrie jumped in before she could say anything further. "You tell me something before you start analyzing my life. What's going on with you and Eddie? That comment you made about the perfume is—I don't know— the second or third one you've made like that."

Jeannie stared at her for a moment, her usually good-natured expression impassive, as if she had suddenly closeted all her feelings. "I was hoping you didn't notice," she said finally.

"I noticed and you're not going to tell me, are you?" Carrie said softly.

Jeannie swallowed. "Why don't you come to the dance tonight?"

Not wanting to push Jeannie to talk until she was ready, Carrie didn't persist. There was something there, something Jeannie didn't want to tell her or ask her. Something deep and hurtful that she was glossing over with her usual good humor. *Eddie likes to look—but not at me...* Jeannie had said that and then sloughed it off as if she'd been joking. Maybe she wasn't joking. Maybe things were worse than anyone knew.

"Okay, I'll come," Carrie said, breaking their eye contact to pick up the stack of résumés she'd finished collating.

"You're easy," Jeannie said lightly.

"You're not too bad yourself," Carrie murmured, putting the pile of papers on one of the end tables in the living room. "You know. I could use a secretary. In fact, what I really need is a wife. Do you remember, by the way, that idea was the whole underpinning of the *Sexy Lady* campaign—that women should stop thinking of themselves as wives or secretaries or executives or mothers and just turn loose the sexy lady inside them."

"I loved those ads, especially the image of the sexy lady emerging from her working-woman clothes. Was that yours?"

Carrie nodded. "It increased sales instantly. I loved those ads. We wanted women no matter what else they did in their lives to feel as if there were another, more powerful woman inside them that they could let out by just wearing that perfume and the right state of mind."

"Oh. Well. The perfume part is easy. How do you get the mindset?"

"There are ways," Carrie said teasingly.

"You sound as if you did research."

"I did research," Carrie said. "We even did a little promo piece for it that we called *Secrets of the Sexy Lady*, and we had it bound into every women's magazine before we hit the market. It was fabulous. It sold like crazy."

"Got any extras?" Jeannie asked.

"I think I do. Actually, I could use a refresher course myself."

"Was that before or after...what was his name?"

"Elliott. Long before. I think the sexy-lady thing must have come with an expiration date or something because I was like Silly Putty in his hands. He just bounced me from pillar to post. Hang on a second, I'll go dig around for it. Why don't you make some coffee?" Carrie went into the den, and rummaged through the box that held all her old ad projects.

Jeannie had a tray waiting on the coffee table when Carrie came in from the den, and she was curled up on the ancient sofa, sipping from her cup.

"Okay. So here's the condition—" Carrie poured her

own cup, and then settled back against the cushions. "You have to *do* these things because that's what changes how you think and feel about yourself."

"I'm game," Jeannie murmured, but she wasn't so sure. Doing sexy things required a certain amount of courage, and she wasn't certain, after all this time, that she had any left. Still, it was a relief that Carrie had figured out that something was wrong without her having to voice it, and a comfort that she could share her burden. "There aren't any guarantees, are there?"

Carrie scanned the booklet. "Nope. And some of the tips sound hopelessly sexist. But this was five or six years ago, so that's a consideration. Okay, here goes.

"The copy says, *'There's a sexy lady inside every woman... She's there in the deepest part of your femininity, and in your consciousness, your body, your soul. She's the woman every woman yearns to be—tantalizing, seductive, sexy...you—'*"

"So far so good," Jeannie murmured.

"*'From time immemorial, certain women have exemplified the secrets of the sexy lady. And now we've researched them, distilled them, and are pleased to present them to you so that you might emerge from your cocoon the sexy lady you were always meant to be.'*"

"Will it hurt?" Jeannie asked.

"Probably," Carrie said. "I'll just further edit these down to the nut of the idea, okay? You can read the rest later. And anyway, most of these are obvious. Like wearing sexy underwear. Do you?"

"Do I what?"

"Wear sexy underthings."

"Do you?"

"Hmm. Not recently. I haven't been in the mood.

However, for the proper mindset, we certainly need to do that tonight."

"I outgrew mine," Jeannie said, her voice quivering a little.

"No problem. Didn't I bring trunks full of clothes from my other life?"

"But I'm not a size ten."

"Yeah. Well. Neither am I anymore. Let's see. It says, sexy ladies wear formfitting clothing. I like that. And no pants. Jeans are abolished as of now."

"What are you going to do? What does it say about leather?"

"I hadn't thought about it. Okay. We have sexy lingerie and formfitting clothes. Of course, I'm bypassing the full philosophy but basically the sexy lady wants to get noticed."

"Exactly," Jeannie said feelingly.

"And let's see, remember that a bosom always commands attention so thank God for the new cleavage bras. Put two of those on the shopping list, preferably made out of silk and lace. Are you keeping a checklist? Is there a naughty-lingerie store anywhere within fifty miles of here?"

Jeannie laughed. "We can get anything our little old hearts desire in Portland."

"That's good. To go on, it says, *'The sexy lady knows that to get attention, she must pay attention, because she knows there's nothing sexier than a good listener. The sexy lady knows that there is nothing more commanding than looking someone straight in the eye, and she makes sure that hers are smoldering with her secret knowledge. The sexy lady expects to get everything that she wants. She tries new things to enhance her desirability and embraces every facet of her sensuality. The sexy lady is bold in the boudoir.'"*

"Is that before or after she removes the lacy lingerie?" Jeannie joked.

"'*The sexy lady knows how to make a man remember*—' Oh, well, enough of that," Carrie said, stopping abruptly. "We're going to make you into a sexy lady tonight, Miss Jeannie."

"Oh yeah? How, with my bulky body and your skimpy clothes?"

"How? There is some good advice in this little pamphlet, and *we* are going to take it."

"You're damn right *we* are going to take it," Jeannie said. "Because I'm not doing anything unless you do it too."

CARRIE FELT as if she was seventeen again as she and Jeannie threw clothes and underwear all around her bedroom.

"So everyone will be wearing jeans and we'll be in skirts and cleavage," Jeannie grumbled as she tried on one blouse after another.

"Listen. You're not that much bigger than I am. You are fine, and there's nothing wrong with looking like a lady for a change. Come on. Get with the program here. The whole point is, if you look different, you'll feel different."

"And what about you?"

"I'd love to feel different. I'd love to not feel like a failure."

"You didn't fail. You had *circumstances*. And at least you took some control. What can I do?"

"Change your style. For three hours. For one night. What could it hurt? We'll show some leg, some bosom, and pay close attention to whoever comes into our orbit, and Eddie will sit up and take notice. Trust me."

"Who are you going to play sexy lady with?"

"My mirror," Carrie said, holding a skirt up against Jeannie's body. "Remember, I'm doing this for you." But in truth, she wasn't sure that she wasn't doing it for herself as well.

THE GRANGE HALL was right in the middle of town behind the Main Street antique shops and village stores. Music was already blasting into the starry night when Carrie turned into the crowded parking lot.

"I'm not sure this is such a good idea," Jeannie said tentatively.

"Let's just go inside and see what Eddie says."

"He won't notice."

"He'll notice," Carrie said firmly, turning off the ignition. "It's just you haven't worn a skirt in so long, you don't know what to do with your legs."

"Yeah. Maybe."

"Look, the real key is the pay-attention part, and getting what you expect. So you'd better aim high, Jeannie, because I expect Eddie to hustle you out of there inside an hour."

"A nice fantasy, Carrie."

"Well, visualize. The mind is very powerful. And you've been underutilizing your power. Come on." Carrie swung out of the car and purposefully went around to Jeannie's side and opened her door. "Let's go, let's go, let's go..."

"It sounded better when you were reading about it," Jeannie muttered. "Okay, I'm coming." She felt naked even though she was smartly and thoroughly clothed. It was just that Carrie's wardrobe didn't run to T-shirts, denims, and sneakers.

Carrie had found a stretchy bodysuit with a surplice

neckline that fit her, and they'd paired that with a long gauzy button-down skirt that revealed a lot of leg, and a pair of sandals. Jeannie had to admit wearing more sophisticated clothes did make her feel different; and they weren't *too* outrageous, she consoled herself as she and Carrie climbed the steps to the hall. Of course, everyone probably expected that kind of thing from Carrie, who'd always had a reputation for dressing conspicuously. But *her?*

Okay. She had to change that kind of thinking. Carrie had drilled it into her. The attitude tonight was not *I can't.* She was supposed to be visualizing *I can and I will. I can and I will walk into the crowd and expect that people are going to react positively to me.*

"Hey Jeannie. Wow, you look nice."

"Jeeeaannnieee—how you doin'?"

"Jeannie—come on over..."

She turned and caught Carrie's eye. Carrie grinned and waved her on.

In the center of the hall, the musicians were taking a break and the crowd was milling around waiting for the start of the next set.

"Jeannie...let me look at you—"

Carrie heard the affection in their voices as everyone called out to Jeannie, beloved, kind, gentle Jeannie who had been part of the community her whole life.

Who couldn't love Jeannie?

What the hell was wrong with Eddie?

Jeannie grabbed her arm. "He's over there," she whispered. "Near the bandstand. Surrounded as usual."

Carrie stared at him. Fifteen years had put weight on Eddie Gerardo, and diminished some of his hair. But otherwise, like Jeannie, he hadn't changed much. He was still affable, sociable and flashy, and she still didn't like him. He owned the real-estate business in town, and he and Jeannie were comfortable but obviously not close. Carrie couldn't help wondering if this was what her life would have been like if she had married young and stayed in town.

I could never have borne all this unhappiness the way Jeannie has, and they have no children, either, after all this time...

"Oh, here's Dr. Tom Kelsey," Jeannie said suddenly. "He's the new vet in town. Hey, Tom, come meet Carrie Spencer."

"Hi." He held out his hand. Tom had a very firm handshake and deep blue eyes. Carrie liked him instantly. "Welcome back."

"So even the newcomers know about the town pariah," Carrie said.

"Actually, it was in the Paradise paper. You know, the list of summer people already in residence. I just happened to read it because I had an ad right on that page." He smiled at her disarmingly before he turned to Jeannie. "You look great."

"Thanks."

Carrie dug her arm into Jeannie's side.

"So do you," Jeannie added, fixing him with an intense look.

"Would you like to dance?" he asked as the musicians mounted the stage.

"Uh..."

Carrie pinched her.

"Yes."

Two of the band members played a long get-ready note on their fiddles, and couples began pairing up.

"Don't tell me that's Truck on stage," Carrie said in surprise.

"Oh yes. He learned to play at college." Jeannie

grabbed Tom's arm. "See you." They whirled off onto the floor with other tapping, bumping, twirling couples, and Carrie edged back to the sidelines to watch Truck as he sawed away at his fiddle and stomped all over the stage.

Why am I watching him? No, I'm watching Jeannie, who's a really good dancer. And Dr. Tom seems to like her, maybe a little too much.

Tom was a lot taller than Jeannie, and he had his arm around her at that point as they two-stepped around the room. Jeannie looked both fragile and happy.

"Is that *Jeannie?*" a voice demanded at her elbow.

Eddie. He sounded a little amazed, and not his usual smooth self.

She turned to look at him. "Hi, Eddie, nice to see you too, and yes, that's Jeannie."

"I thought you two were cooking something up."

"I'd say Jeannie's cooking tonight. She's a terrific dancer."

"Yeah, she likes to come to these things," Eddie said, his attention torn between Jeannie and the two women he had been talking to. "It's not quite the evening out you're probably used to."

"I can get used to anything," Carrie said.

"So they say," Eddie countered. "Well, good to see you, Carrie."

"You too, Eddie," she murmured, not even flinching at his snide comment, and certain he hadn't even heard her as he edged away.

This wasn't going to be easy, she thought. Eddie was not an easy man, and probably now he was too used to the way things were. It was going to take time to shake him up, and determination on Jeannie's part. At least he'd noticed that Jeannie wasn't looking quite the same.

And then she became aware that the music had slowed down appreciably, that Truck wasn't on stage, and before she could decide on a strategy, he came up right beside her.

"Care to dance?"

"I knew this would happen."

"So did I. So what's your point?"

"I'm lending Jeannie moral support. I'm not supposed to have a good time."

"Oh." That devastating smile again. "Okay, dance with me and don't enjoy it."

"I'm not going to *do* this," Carrie said firmly. Truck had no business coming after her. She wasn't interested, especially after witnessing Eddie's flagrant indifference to Jeannie. That was what married life usually came to: a fragmented relationship held together by the tenuous strings of companionship, and sorely frayed without the glue of a family.

Not for me...

"You don't have to do anything, just dance with me."

"You said that yesterday too."

"Did I? This isn't a lifetime commitment, Carrie. It's ten minutes on the dance floor."

And in your arms. She braced herself as he slipped his arm around her and took her hand.

"I know how you are," he murmured as she wrestled with him for control. "This is just the slow dance."

"Right. You think I don't know what that means. I know what that slow-dance business means, Truck."

"It means we're dancing slowly, Carrie. To the beat. Step together step. We learned it in high school. What do you think it means?"

It meant he was holding her too tight, too right, too close. He knew just how, just the way she liked it. They moved together as if they'd been doing it forever, and that was scary too.

"Don't think," Truck murmured. "Just...dance—" He pulled her more tightly against him. Step together step, in perfect sync, her hips moving to the beat, moving against him where he fit so perfectly against her. She was made for him, he was convinced of it, and she wasn't immune to him either, on any level. He sent a covert signal to the band, and the music played on. Couples dropped out, regrouped, and returned to the dance floor with new partners. He held her still closer, enveloping her in his heat, moving his hands to enfold her more intimately.

"I have to—Jeannie..." Carrie murmured.

"Jeannie's fine. Tom is right there, and Eddie's prowling the sidelines. You can't do anything right now, Carrie. At least not for Jeannie."

"Oh yeah? Who for, then?" she asked combatively.

"How about you?"

"I'm fine, thank you, and getting as tired as the band must be. Why don't you have mercy on them and let them stop?"

"Not until I see you pushing and grinding and twining. In fact..."

"Truck—"

"Here we go..." The music changed, fast as lightning. Lines formed all around them with hopping, stomping dancers, and Truck swung her around and pushed her into the line.

It was one of those sink-or-swim moments; she saw instantly that she'd be a step or two behind everyone else, and way out of her element, but she was game anyway.

Carrie saw Jeannie talking to a tall fair man, her gaze

intent, her body language fairly radiating confidence. She saw Eddie along the sidelines trying to keep track of Jeannie and several other of his women friends. She was very aware of Truck beside her, and the moves and kicks and thrusts of the dance, and how good he was at moving and thrusting.

She stopped dead on the floor. Was there never a moment when she wasn't thinking about him in sexual terms? Why was she thinking about him *at all?* She almost bolted. *It's just a dance, Carrie. There are sixty people on this floor. Sixty neighbors. What do you think is going to happen?*

The music wound down and everyone applauded and went in search of refreshments. Truck took her arm and guided her off the floor. "Lemonade?"

"Please."

"Here comes Jeannie," he remarked, grasping Jeannie's hand and squeezing it as she passed him.

"Hey," Carrie murmured.

"Uplift works," Jeannie said excitedly, pulling her aside.

"No kidding."

"Eddie can't figure out what's different. I can't thank you—"

Carrie held up her hand. "Hold it, Jeannie. This isn't a done deal with Eddie. This is an ongoing process. It's going to take a lot of time and effort...and attitude."

"I know, I know."

"And patience."

"I know...but he's taking me home. Usually he stays and I go home alone. Don't you think that's meaningful?"

"I think you confused him tonight. At least two men

that I saw were very attentive to you, and I'm guessing that doesn't always happen."

"Oh, it happens. He just never notices."

"You should go home with him then. I'll get someone to take me home."

"Okay. Sometime this week I want to go shopping."

"It's a date."

Jeannie squeezed her hand and flew across the dance floor as the band started warming up again. Eddie waited for her by the door. He entwined his arm with hers as they exited, and Carrie watched skeptically.

It was a hard thing to watch, Jeannie's pain, then her sudden hope. Maybe she'd done her a disservice. All the sexy-lady business was nothing more than a bandage over long-festering wounds that Carrie knew nothing about. Didn't want to know anything about. She wasn't going to be here long enough to get involved. Eventually, all she could do for Jeannie was leave her behind, and everything else. *Everyone else.*

"So Jeannie's gone home." Truck handed her a paper cup of lemonade. "And I take it you're stranded."

Carrie sipped. "Stranded? I don't know if I'd put it that strongly. I bet I could find someone to take me home."

"I dare you to let me."

"I'm not scared of you, Truck."

"Sure you are, but that's okay. A kiss isn't a commitment either."

"But you'll do it again, then where will I be?"

"Soundly and thoroughly kissed, and what's so bad about that?"

Carrie didn't like where the conversation was going. "Don't you have a date with a fiddle?" she said.

"Nope. I'm going to stay right here and burn. Come on, Carrie. You're making more of this than it is."

No, I'm not. And if I were smart, I would not walk one foot out the door with him.

I'm not smart. And uplift works.

Tom rescued her. "How about it, Carrie?"

She took his hand. "I'd love to."

It was so much easier to follow Tom. He held her politely, nicely, and his conversation was easy and humorous. He was in fact a very nice man, young, enthusiastic and a great advocate for the quality of life that had been the draw that brought him to Paradise from Chicago.

He wondered hopefully if she had a pet.

"There are some outdoor cats hanging around, so I can't really promise you any business," Carrie said regretfully. "Nor am I sure how long I'll be staying in town."

"You'll stay," Tom predicted. "You'll see. Thanks, Carrie," he said as he brought her back to Truck.

"Thank you," she said warmly. He was halfway across the floor when it occurred to her that he probably would have been very happy to give her a lift home.

"He would've," Truck said, reading her mind as he sidled up to her. "But he's no fun."

He swung her into the next dance, another slow dance, before she could protest. And then it was too late to push away, and by that time Carrie didn't want to, anyway.

Uplift was dangerous. Men could detect uplift a mile away. She would bet Truck knew exactly what she was wearing under her thin silk shirt. And she was too aware of the softness of her body against the hardness of his as she moved against him.

This was dangerous. This was stupid. Why was her

body warring with her common sense? Why was her body winning?

She pulled away. "Truck..."

He pulled her back firmly. "Carrie," he mimicked her tone. "Let's just do one dance at a time."

"You don't get to choreograph everything," Carrie muttered.

"No, but *I* get to lead."

She wanted to bite him. For an instant, her mind was flooded with images: her lips on his shoulder, his chest, his belly...lower—*no!*

She shook herself. She had to stop thinking like this.

She needed a healthy dose of that sexy-lady attitude, she thought. Elusive would be good. And cool. Calm. All the things she wasn't right now, with Truck's long lean body molded to hers.

Why did he still have the power to affect her like this? Carrie felt as if she was on the verge of something explosive, something that would change her forever.

No, if she had given herself to him all those years ago, that would have changed her forever. Would have changed her life forever.

She hadn't come back home to shake up her life. She didn't want complications. And she didn't want to start anything with Truck, not after all this time. And especially not after Elliott.

Well, the sexy lady should be able handle that, she thought. She'd just push it to one side and never think about it again. And she'd curl Truck McKelvey right around her little finger and keep her emotions neatly disengaged.

But that was the fantasy. The reality was that the music was too hot, Truck was too close and she was too susceptible.

Carrie became aware suddenly that the music had

stopped and he was still holding her tightly and swaying in a rhythm she felt right down to her toes.

It would be so easy, too easy to let go...

"Come on," he murmured against her ear. "I'll take you home."

There wasn't any graceful way out of that either. He was already at a slow simmer and halfway out the door, and she wasn't far behind.

But—the sexy lady could deal with that. It was all a matter of attitude. She could be detached. Not a problem, she thought resolutely. The sexy lady would know just how to handle Truck. Now, if only she could get a handle on how Truck was making her feel.

5

TRUCK DROVE a meticulously restored thirty-year-old Mercedes sedan luxuriously appointed with burled wood, leather and ivory. An executive's car, Carrie thought, smooth, quiet, unobtrusive, elegant.

Surprising.

It occurred to Carrie that she didn't know Truck at all, and that the way he handled this car would be very much the way he would handle a woman: with a gentle touch, and with passion and control.

She shivered. She felt out of control. There wasn't anything about him that didn't remind her of the past or make her think of possibilities in the present. It was too much, too soon. And all those feelings overrode any common-sense response she might have had to the situation. Her plans didn't include this. She didn't want this.

Where was that disdainful sexy lady who knew just how to say no? She was whispering in Carrie's ear, goading her to say *yes*. Except Truck hadn't asked her anything yet. It was just in the air, in the closeness of the car, in the jolting knowledge between them. There were some things you couldn't escape. Some things that were meant to happen. Some things that endured.

"Did you ever wonder," Truck said as he maneuvered the Mercedes down the track toward her house, "what would have happened if we'd made love?"

She'd wondered that endlessly those first years in college. Sometimes, even after she'd gone to New York, though she'd been certain that she had made the right decision.

"No," Carrie said.

"Liar."

"Does it matter?"

"You tell me," Truck said, swinging the car at an angle to the pond and cutting the engine.

"Did it matter to you?" she asked curiously.

He was silent a long moment. "It did."

"Because you didn't make it with me and everyone thought you'd be the one who did?" Carrie said, unable to keep the caustic tone out of her voice.

"No," he said gently. "Actually I thought we were in love. But then, you had four guys snapping at your heels those last two years of school. I just happened to be the one who got closest."

No, you happened to be the one I really wanted...

"Why are we raking over old memories?" she asked, discomfited by his honesty. They had never ever talked about love.

Love...

"I thought you might have some regrets."

No. Yes. Maybe. "I don't regret anything," she said a bit too firmly as if she had to convince herself as much as she did Truck.

"No," he murmured, making a move toward her. The move she feared, the move she wanted. "This is better."

"Don't you dare kiss me."

"Then you kiss me, Carrie."

"I knew I should've stayed home."

"No Carrie." He moved closer to her. "I think... you've finally...*come* home..."

He touched her mouth gently, achingly, with his own. "Say yes, Carrie."

"I don't," she responded reluctantly, pulling back slowly from the pressure of his too-seductive lips, "want to..."

"Yes, you do." He settled his mouth on hers again. He didn't probe, he didn't seek, he didn't push. He was just there, feeling the texture of her lips, tasting them, nipping them lightly. "It's only a kiss..."

Only.

"You keep saying that," she murmured as he took her lips again, forcefully this time, sinking himself into the deepest recesses of her mouth before she could protest.

Don't keep saying that...

Oh, but keep doing that...and that—

*And that—*as he took her into the heat and the storm of his mouth.

His long strong fingers dug into her thick hair to position her at just the angle he needed to plunder her.

His hands were so strong, his mouth so insistent. She wanted to run, she wanted to stay, and he had always evoked that feeling in her because the trap was those kisses, those hands, that body, and all the possibilities that existed for heartbreak.

Or love.

But love had nothing to do with it.

Or this. This was...just a kiss. Only a kiss. A never-ending kiss going deeper and darker and searing her soul.

"Truck..." She could barely breathe, barely speak, and his lips hovered a scant breath above hers, waiting, waiting... Had he always been waiting?

"Carrie," he murmured in the same tone. He knew what was coming: the warrior princess in ambivalent mode. She wanted him, didn't. Couldn't. Wouldn't. And anyway...he'd heard the whole story fifteen years before. And he'd bought it, and stupidly, he'd let her get away.

Not this time. He was so much more patient now.

"This is not *just* a kiss," Carrie said huskily.

"What is it then?"

"I'm not going to let you do this, Truck."

"What am I doing?"

"Trading on memories, damn you."

"I don't remember anything like this, actually," he murmured.

"You don't remember making out in a car?"

"Is that what we're talking about? Wasn't it the back of the truck? And anyway," he added, usurping her line, "what's that got to do with this...?"

Truck then slowly angled his mouth on hers again and shifted his weight purposefully against her body. No matter what she said, she wanted those kisses.

She felt as if there were two of her—the self-protective Carrie who didn't want to get entangled with men anymore who could break her heart; and the sexy lady who took everything she could get and still maintained her distance.

There was no distance between her and Truck, and his heat, his scent, his need.

And hers.

Where had that come from?

Where...? From those clever, clever hands purposefully touching her in the places her heart remembered.

Her awareness came slowly as he distracted her mouth and tongue with bone-melting kisses and slowly and lightly began stroking her all over with his fingers.

All the places he knew so well and hadn't forgotten:

the underside of her earlobe, the base of her neck, the crook of her arm, her midriff, and the most lethal place of all—the undercurve of her breast. Her insides turned liquid as she felt his fingers slide along the underside of her breast. She wanted to push him away, she wanted him to forget, to never stop, to take her there and then, because the sensations were so powerful and over- whelming, she didn't know what else to do with them.

And he knew it. This part of Carrie he had always known, and this part he could touch so easily through the light-as-air clothing she wore. But what part could he touch to make her wholly and completely his? Truck wanted to envelop her, to imprint her so that no one else would ever touch her again. Carrie was made for him, he'd known it fifteen years before, and the feeling was that much more magnified as she fought her need to melt into his arms.

A man had to have a battle plan. And a thorough, honed-in-the-crucible knowledge of his adversary.

"Come to me, Carrie," he whispered as he nudged her onto her lap. "Come." He pulled her gently so that she unwillingly straddled his legs.

"*Just* a kiss," she murmered as she braced herself against his shoulders.

She was on top now, she thought fuzzily, she could just open the car door and go into the house. And maybe he had done that deliberately because he knew she wouldn't want to go once she was at the mercy of his wicked magic hands.

And those kisses.

She couldn't leave those kisses. Her control, her deci- sion. Her body liquefied as she sought his mouth avidly and claimed him.

Just a kiss...

He slipped his hands under her skirt and up her bare thighs to the outer curve of her buttocks where she most liked to be caressed.

That too...oh, especially that—

He released the car seat into a reclining position so that she was fully stretched out against him, and he was nestled tightly between her legs.

Now Truck had full play of her lower body, which was clothed in a next-to-nothing wisp of bikini panty, and he intended to use every weapon in his arsenal to make her come—to him and for him.

Carrie felt his hands working on her buttocks in a delicious circular motion and she pulled abruptly out of the kiss.

"Don't stop," he murmured.

"You stop."

"Don't want to."

"Because...?"

"You love this."

"Maybe not," she said fretfully, but her body betrayed her and she pressed closer, inviting him to explore further. Not a smart thing to do because the motion of his hands only intensified the roiling excitement in her.

She wanted to close her eyes and give in to it. Why not? They were not teenagers anymore, and yet there was an overlay of that emotion, that discovery on the edge of surrender.

But this time, she thought as she undulated against the expert manipulation of those magic fingers, this time she would know what she was getting into, she'd know how to handle it.

This time, she could give in to the fantasy and not get hurt.

This time...

She wanted to. This time—

"Too many maybes, Carrie. How about something definitive? Yes, I love this will do." He moved his hands and cupped her buttocks.

Her eyes closed; her body caved. His hands were so big, so knowing, so there. He knew her so intimately, and she knew him. And she was too aware of the compressed power of him lodged so tightly between her legs.

"Say yes," he whispered.

All that thrust and motion just for her. All that explosive need focused solely in her. The thought turned her limbs to jelly.

The air grew thicker, closer. She felt him sliding his hands to forbidden places. *Yes.* She reacted tellingly, her body shuddering as she enticed him to probe still more. *Yes.*

She didn't know if she said it out loud, *yes*, but he knew, he knew.

All she had to do was surrender to his kisses, to his hands, and let him submerge her in his power and his passion.

She was drowning already. And practically naked, with her silk and gauze outfit drifting across the seat beside her. He moved subtly so as not to break the kiss, baring his soul, enshrouding his desire, and then he surged against her, hot for her and seeking her in the most elemental way.

She just wanted to lie against the pure raw power of him, to feel his length, his heat, against her body. She wanted to touch him, play with him, fit herself around him.

All of those emotions and more swirled in her as she wedged her body against the ridge of his gorgeous erection. She remembered this—oh, how she remembered this. He was unforgettable, as long and hard in his maleness as he was in body and soul.

She wanted Truck. He had been everything she'd wanted back then—and strong, decisive and good looking besides.

What she hadn't known then was how she could have him and everything else too. So she had said no. No, she had said to his kisses and his coaxing. No, at that one shimmering moment when he'd been primed for possession and she'd been ready, needy, wanting. No, no, and no, she had said, and for five years afterward she had lived with the pain, the remorse, the sorrow, and worse, the regret of not knowing what it would have been like to have Truck make love to her.

This time, she wouldn't say no.

This time...

This time it was he who shifted her body, guiding her surely and elegantly with those knowing hands, and giving himself into her control, her desire and her hands for the moment of penetration.

She grasped him firmly with a sure knowledge of what he still loved, what he still wanted, and what her touch would do to him. She held every last hard pulsating inch of him in her hands and inches away from heaven.

"Carrie..." His voice was strangled.

"I know." She cradled him between her hands, sliding them up and down the shaft, feeling every nuance of him. "I know," she whispered as she positioned him and as she took him inch by throbbing inch deep and hard into her body.

The connection was breathtaking and powerful. She felt as if she were permanently joined to him as she braced herself against his thighs. She didn't want to move. She didn't want to speak.

"Carrie…"

She made a helpless little sound at the back of her throat.

He had to be strong for both of them. She was so tight and hot and ready for him, and all he could do was grasp her hands and pull her forward so he could kiss her. He tasted tears on her vulnerable mouth. He tasted regret, need and desire and everything he'd ever wanted to know about her.

"Come for me, Carrie," he murmured against her lips. He surged against her, anchoring himself even more deeply in her. "Come…"

She didn't want to move. She wanted him within her forever, and she was shaken to the core by these feelings. This wasn't the simple coupling of a one-night stand. This was something deeper, much more serious, and she felt as if she couldn't bear for it to end.

But he could only contain himself for so long. Even he, with his infinite patience and devastating control, had a breaking point, and he was almost there. But then she moved, just a ripple of her body, and it told him everything. She was ready now, and he undulated against her, finding her center and seeking her mouth in a kiss that exploded into heat and urgency.

He gripped her hips then, initiating a rhythmic movement that he met with short hard pumping thrusts into her slick sleek body, aiming perfectly at her sensual soul.

And that pleasure point became her world, and the heat and wet of his kisses, and the scent of the leather, and the sultry evening air. All of that seeped into her pores, enfolding her in the universe of his body, his hunger, his sex.

She felt the very moment that they became one, when she lost the sensation of her body in the length and thrust of his, one body, one motion joined at the most exquisite point, and then gone, gone, gone almost before she knew it in a flare of shimmering light that blazed through her body and erupted like a depth charge.

It was volcanic, unexpected, utterly consuming him.

They lay very still for a very long time, Carrie enfolded in his arms, and his face buried in her tumbled hair.

Too fast, too far, he thought. Not enough time. Not enough play. Not a great place. Too many "nots" for something so perfect.

And so perfect, there was room for nothing more.

IT WAS DONE. Her curiosity was satisfied, her body sated. She wasn't in love, Carrie decided. She might be in lust, because Truck was too perfect, even in the awkward confines of a car, but she wasn't going to spend her time thinking about that, or him. The end was anticlimactic. All the excitement, all the feelings eddied away in the getting dressed, saying good-night, cumbersome moments that seemed to diminish what they had shared.

It was fine, Carrie thought. She was still heart-whole. He didn't have to call to reassure her, even though he said he would. She knew what the promise to call meant in the world of tenuous one-night stands.

They were adults, she said, brushing it off. She was fine.

But he did call the very next morning, to tell her he was off on a week-long emergency-service call to repair a ruptured pipeline all the way up to Searsport. He'd see her on the weekend.

He was letting her down easy, Carrie thought. It was

almost as if the intensity of what they'd shared had scared him off. It was better that way.

Besides, she had work to do. There were more résumés to send, letters to write, and searching the Internet job banks.

And at the weekend, there was a treat—she and Jeannie were going shopping on Saturday. Jeannie wanted to do the whole sexy-lady shopping spree, and Carrie was happy to go along to Portland, then maybe up to Freeport. Jeannie was to come early Saturday so they could make a list.

"I mean, I really liked how I felt in that outfit you put together," Jeannie had said when she'd called in the afternoon to propose the trip. "All I wear to work is dark blue suits with skirts. There isn't much leeway for sexy stuff there."

"Except underwear," Carrie had pointed out, "which can be a big turn-on for some men."

"Well, we're not working with *some* men here. And this man has grown too accustomed to me and my face. And I don't think he's really seen my body in years."

"He saw it last night."

"Right. And I want to shake him up even more."

"It's your dollar," Carrie had said.

"And yours. I don't do it unless you do, remember."

"Right," Carrie had said. As if she had any kind of spare change to expend on becoming a sexy lady. She'd had about all she could handle last week anyway.

"Nine o'clock," Jeannie had said.

"I'll be here."

In the meantime, Carrie went to the bank, bought groceries, read the Portland papers and worked on her portfolio while sitting on the porch relishing the beauty of the landscape.

The pond was quiet during the week. Sometimes, in the morning, she would awaken to the cackling of a loon, and ducks were everywhere thanks to everyone on the pond offering them food.

Friday night, when the weekend and summer residents were in town, the noise level ratcheted up as motorboats swooped over the water from house to house in an ongoing outdoor party, and voices carried across the water: the sound of greetings and goodbyes, loud laughter, louder conversation.

The blackflies were long gone by then, and nights sometimes were autumn-like. Her mother had always kept an electric blanket on hand for the coolish summer nights. Or a down comforter.

Small comfort now, Carrie thought. *I need my mother.*

A spasm of grief rocketed through her body, ambushing her out of nowhere. Again.

Why had she thought she was done grieving?

Of course you'll go to college, dear. Of course you can go away. No use staying here if you don't want to. It's rather nice for me, actually, with all my friends and my volunteer work and the church. And the house is so cozy...

Carrie shivered and swiped at her tears.

We were so lucky to find a nice place to live after everything we've been through. Dry your tears, dear. Everything will work out fine. I trust you. You won't make the same mistakes. It will kill me if all this was for nothing. You know...you know...you know...

Her mother's voice echoing against all those futile years she had sacrificed so that Carrie could go forth, take risks and be a success.

And where had Carrie wound up? Right back at the beginning.

Paradise. For her mother, it had been exactly that, a

haven to escape a brutal life after her father had died. There had been no money, no family, no sympathy, no friends. Just one ragged lonely unskilled woman driven to provide safety and security for one small child.

How had her mother done it? She had taken in sewing. She had cleaned the houses of the summer residents and people around the Pond.

It had been subsistance living, enough to pay a minimal rent on a broken-down house no one else had wanted. Enough so that she had been able to slowly and painstakingly make repairs. And enough to have sent a daughter through college with the help of a scholarship. Enough so her mother had ultimately been able to buy the place she had called home.

And Carrie had never known. Had never asked. Had just taken it for granted that was the way things were.

She wiped away her tears. This was ridiculous. She was getting emotional because...well, because.

Truck had nothing to do with it. He'd had his shot and he was gone, and it was nothing less than she expected. She'd dealt with guys like that for years, guys who loved the chase and thought that seeing someone for more than one night was tantamount to commitment.

At least Truck had actually called. It was definitely a point in his favor, but she was the one who would pay the dearest price, because memory and desire had already coalesced into the fierce need to see him again.

To be with him.

Which only proved she needed that whole sexy-lady shopping spree more than Jeannie, because she still hadn't learned how to hold a man at arm's length while taking everything he had to give.

She called Jeannie. "Forget Saturday morning. You'd

better come over Friday night, because I want to devote *hours* to making up that shopping list."

THEY STARTED OUT early Saturday morning for Portland with the intention of hitting every specialty shop and department store before heading up to Freeport and the discount designer shops. Not that Carrie had any money to spend, but she did have a list.

Jeannie, however, had a list, a credit card and more determination than Carrie could ever remember seeing in her.

"Did you discover the secret of sex or something?" Carrie asked curiously. "I've never seen you like this."

"No. It's nothing more or less than I told you. New clothes for a newly minted sexy lady."

"Maybe we're carrying this a little too far," Carrie said.

"Or maybe not far enough," Jeannie said, zipping through the toll station and onto the turnpike. "Besides, it'll be fun. You need a day out. You're looking just a little tense."

"Nothing much is happening." *Nothing. Period. And Truck didn't count.*

"Story of my life," Jeannie muttered. "No. Forget that. I'm going to stop saying things like that."

They found parking a half hour later on the streets of Old Port, and spent an hour wandering down the narrow streets, in and out of the shops, looking at crafts, books, jewelry and antiques.

Fabulous little shops, Carrie thought, that might need someone to do a little freelance ad work for them— maybe get ads in those tourist newspapers that were distributed in supermarkets all over New England. Maybe, if there was enough interest, the store owners could publish one of their own, or do a co-op insert in all the surrounding community papers. And the outlet malls. Maybe...

She caught herself. Maybe—she was thinking as if there were possibilities here. As if she intended to stay. But she wasn't ready to admit that. She wasn't ready for anything except breakfast, and certainly not cold calls down a road that would probably lead nowhere.

"This is not getting much of our list done," she said over coffee when they finally stopped to eat. "Wait till Eddie sees those big bold pieces of jewelry you bought."

"The sexy lady *is* bold, is she not? Tell the truth—you wrote the copy."

"But she's always a lady," Carrie said.

"I think these pieces are very tasteful," Jeannie said, holding up one necklace, a swoop of silver, to her neck. "This will look great with a suit and a silk blouse. Of course, I need a silk blouse. I've been wearing cotton. Oxford. Can you get any more boring than that?"

"Okay, but just don't go overboard here, Jeannie," Carrie cautioned. "This isn't going to change anything but *you*." And point of fact, she wondered if Jeannie was giving herself up at the expense of feeling better. But maybe she really needed a minimakeover. Maybe everyone who had been married as long as Jeannie had to rumble a little. Maybe she would have too, if she'd stayed in Paradise and gotten married.

Carrie shook off the thought. She had her own wardrobe of silk blouses, designer suits and gold jewelry and it had changed nothing. It was just the outer layer, the presentation. Every veneer cracked under pressure; no one was immune, even her. Witness her escapade with Truck.

Truck... She hadn't changed one iota in fifteen years.

She felt as if she was still waiting for his call. Stop it, she told herself.

"Okay, Jeannie, your call—where do we go next?"

Jeannie's eyes lit up. "Lingerie. I want a heap of silk and lace to replace all my cotton and flannel. What do you sleep in?"

Carrie laughed. "An oversize T-shirt. Not very sexy lady, I'm afraid."

"I bet you have one of those nightgowns—you know the ones—they sell 'em in catalogs and they only fit you if you're a size two..."

"In my drawer. Still in the box. Don't go nuts and start romanticizing my life. It's pretty much been on a career track and there hasn't been much time for anything else."

"Except—what was his name? Elliott."

"We don't talk about Elliott anymore," Carrie said brusquely. "That was another life, another place." And she didn't want to talk about Truck either. *That* too was another life, another place. And it was over before it got started while she was panting for more.

"All right," Jeannie said as she expertly steered into a parking slot close to one of the entrances at the vast Vacationland Mall. She knew when a subject was off-limits. At least for the moment. "Here we go."

Then it was just one store after another, the packages piling up as if Jeannie was buying Christmas presents.

"You have to buy one of those cleavage bras," she told Carrie, taking bold charge of the situation and steering them into the store with the lingerie secrets. "My treat."

"I think I can still afford a piece of underwear," Carrie said dryly.

They tried on everything—the bras, the little nothing panties in every shape from bikini cut to thong, then all the nightgowns and lacy slips, especially the ones with built-in cups, which Jeannie just adored.

She bought three of the cleavage bras, an equal number of slips, five lace-lavished nightgowns in jewel colors that exposed various parts of her body and satin boudoir slides.

Carrie bought a bra and a nightgown just to pacify Jeannie, then they hit the clothing stores.

"Silk first," Jeannie said definitively. "The sexy lady wears clothing that makes men want to touch. I read that in the booklet, by the way."

"I created a monster," Carrie groaned.

"No. You created a new way of thinking about yourself. For me and how many other women who took the advice in the booklet. You did a good thing."

"I wonder."

"Trust me."

Carrie was still wondering by the end of the day. Jeannie had gone overboard, in her opinion. She'd bought new suits, a dozen blouses, all silk, new casual wear, favoring the long button-front skirts in which she could flash some leg, and a dozen bodysuits with different necklines to show off her new cleavage. Shoes were next, sandals, pumps for work, and slightly-higher-than-that heels to wear with everything else.

"Just think of how many years I wasn't buying clothes," Jeannie said cheerfully as they loaded their shopping bags in the trunk of her car. "Do you know how old some of my stuff is?"

"But you're trying to make up for lost time in one day," Carrie pointed out.

"No, I'm trying to make up for letting myself become a *not* sexy lady. And I'm not going to apologize for that.

Besides, you have great taste and I really appreciate your reining me in."

"Not a problem," Carrie said.

"I wish you'd bought more."

"That really would have been a waste of money. I can't wear half the clothes I have now. Plus if I don't get a job, I think I'm going to have to sell them all."

"Think positive," Jeannie counseled. "One small change—it's just like you said, you know. Change one thing. I can't believe how different I feel."

"Only if you're doing it for yourself," Carrie warned her again. "Not if you're doing it for Eddie."

"I'm not," Jeannie said defiantly. "I wanted to feel better—no, differently. And I do. So what's next? Do you think we need to go to Freeport?"

"Only if you want to."

"No, I think I'd rather go home."

Carrie thought she would too. She was tired. She was just a little scared that she had unleashed something in Jeannie that would have far-reaching consequences. And she hadn't yet come to grips with what had happened Saturday night.

While she'd looked forward to the shopping trip to keep from thinking about her encounter with Truck, she found she couldn't stop thinking about it at all, and that Jeannie's company was wearing when she was in this mood.

They made the trip back to Paradise in relative silence. Jeannie's adrenaline rush seemed to have run out. Carrie felt exhausted altogether and drifted into sleep.

Jeannie's voice awakened her. "Truck's at your place."

Carrie bolted into a sitting position. His car was parked on the dirt track to her house. In the distance, she

could hear him hammering on the roof, though he was
obscured by the heavy foliage.

I'll see you on the weekend.

She didn't want this, she didn't.

Side work. That was all it was. All *she* was.

She couldn't let it be anything else.

She took her bags from the trunk of Jeannie's car, and
slowly, she walked down to the house.

6

HE SAW her coming through the trees, a flash of bright blue silk over snug black jeans, her hair piled into a topknot, her arms full of packages. He hadn't seen her for a week and it felt like a year because he'd only had time to make that one phone call to tell her he would be gone.

It had been a rough week on top of that, thirteen hours a day of laying pipeline then falling exhausted into bed. A man didn't have much energy for anything else after that.

He'd dreamed about Carrie the way he had on and off for the last fifteen years. And now here she was, looking like a dream, but real. So real he wanted her more than ever. However, as much as Carrie wanted to run, whatever she might say, she couldn't deny the reality of what had happened between them last Saturday night.

Putting his tools down on the edge of the roof, he shifted on the ladder to get a better look at Carrie. "Hey," he called out.

Carrie shielded her eyes as she looked up at him, even though she was wearing sunglasses. "Hi." Light and casual. She knew how to play the game. "Want something to drink?"

"Sure."

"I'll bring some lemonade out," she said as she unlocked the door and went inside the house.

Okay, that was easy. She dropped her packages in the

bedroom, kicked off her sandals and shoved her feet into a pair of dock shoes, and went to the kitchen to get some lemonade.

He could probably drink a quart, she thought. He'd probably been working on the roof most of the day.

"Come on up," he called as she emerged from the house. "It's wonderful up here."

Carrie hesitated on the first rung of the ladder he had propped against the side of the house and gazed up at him.

A sun god, she thought, golden and burnished from the afternoon sun. She couldn't see his eyes, she couldn't see his face. All she could feel was his intense magnetic pull, and her own reluctant response.

She wanted to be with him.

She was really getting crazy. It had to be the air or the water. This was not in her game plan, making love with Truck McKelvey.

No, but it could be in her afternoon.

Afternoon delight.

Damn, why was she thinking like this?

She shoved the two plastic quart bottles of lemonade in each pocket and mounted the ladder. Truck held out his hand and pulled her up onto the porch roof.

He had made it into a little hidden space for himself. There was a radio softly playing jazz, a blanket on which he'd laid his tools, a lunch box, towels and a bucket of water. To one side, there was a pile of shingles, flashing, roof cement, assorted pipes, couplings, tape and containers of various liquids and pastes. All around them were trees screening out the world and sheltering them from the fierce heat of the sun. Through the trees, Carrie could just see the pond and the opposite shore. A boat here and there, sailing by. Birds chittering. A woodpecker knocking. Ducks quacking.

She looked back over at Truck, his T-shirt grease-spattered and sweaty, and his jeans riding low on his hips. He dipped his hands in the water, and splashed it on his face and hair in a purely male gesture before taking the plastic bottle from her. He held her eyes as he twisted off the cap, saluted her, lifted the bottle to his lips and took the first draw of the lemonade. Her insides coiled, and she had to look away as she opened her own bottle and drank from it.

There was something so compelling about how contained he was, how calm and competent. Yet there was an aura of danger he always radiated.

Truck was a man who should be doing bigger, more exciting things, she thought. He could command boardrooms, he could manage industries. And here he was, rubbing his arms up and down with water and toweling himself off, perfectly content to piece together waste lines and vents.

Carrie didn't understand it. She didn't want to. She felt the drive within her to escape, to live on a larger canvas. She quelled the feeling because there was no escaping the here and now, and if she didn't think about it, she could appreciate the beauty of this moment and this summer day.

This fantasy...

She felt his arm slide around her shoulders as he came up behind her.

"So, what exactly was Saturday night all about?" he murmured in her ear.

"Sex," she said promptly, combatively. It was good she didn't have to look at him, but she was so unnerved by his tanned muscular arm around her, she thought her knees would give out. "You scratched an itch."

"I did?" He sounded amused. "If that's *all* I did, calamine lotion would've worked just as well, Carrie."

He knew damn well that wasn't *all* he'd done, Carrie thought. He'd done too much, was what he'd done, and she didn't know how to cope with it. The feelings he had unleashed in her were too strong, too raw and too tender, and she couldn't keep the image of them together out of her mind.

There was something about the heat of the sun that was making her hot too. And the sight of him, and scent of him so close to her. There was danger here, and a subtle enchantment, and she wasn't immune to it even after all this time.

"Lean against me, Carrie. It won't kill you."

"It will demolish me," she said, knowing it was futile to resist. She was lost already, her whole body shuddering as she backed into the wall of his chest, his erection, the heat of his hunger.

"You're so fragmented," he murmured, touching her left earlobe just where she liked it. "Why don't you let yourself become whole?"

"How?" she whispered, turning her head toward those stroking fingers that were sending little darts of pleasure streaking between her legs.

"Stop fighting."

"Okay, I surrender," she murmured breathlessly.

"Nonsense. You wear your resistance like armor." He moved his arm from around her shoulders to the swell of her breasts and began arcing his fingers over the sensitive curve just above the nipple.

Immediately, she arched her body toward him, demanding more.

Secrets. He knew all her secrets, and he knew exactly how to get past every obstacle, and at that moment, she didn't care.

"I think you just got past my defenses," she whispered barely above a breath, lifting her arms and inviting him to stroke her just there still more.

"I like it when you're soft and willing." He was rubbing both breasts now over the curve, and she thought she would dissolve right in his hands. An insistent little twinge in her body demanded even more.

Soon, she thought, soon. Her excitement escalated. She wanted to be naked for him, with every impediment out of the way, her silky tank, her jeans, her shoes. *Yes,* as his wicked hands claimed breasts again, beneath the support of that uplifting bra. *Yes,* as he tore off her thong panty. *Yes,* as the sun beat down, sultry and hot, and he gently eased her to her knees on the blanket, then quickly pulled off his jeans and T-shirt.

Yes to whatever he wanted...anything he wanted—as long as he kept up the rhythmic stroking over the swell of her breasts.

He came behind her, on his knees. She felt him probing, pushing slowly slowly slowly into her hot center so that she felt every hard inch of him as he entered. She could hardly breathe, she didn't want to move ever again. She felt strong, sexy, invincible.

Truck rocked against her gently, testing her need. She pushed back against him. *Stay there, just there...just—*

She caught her breath as he boldly grasped her hips and thrust himself into her, riding her hard, hot and heavy, mastering her very soul.

And she loved it. She wanted it. Under the hot haze of the summer sun, she couldn't get enough of him, and she teased him and enticed him to give her still more. She was the temptress and he was at her feet, and she would give exactly as much as she wanted to, and take everything she could—

Sexy sexy lady...

Lush sensations unfurled deep within her core—

He is at your mercy—

...almost there, almost there, from the erotic pressure of *him* pushing, goading, demanding she come...almost there—one last thrust, hard, high—and then a stream of sensation that skeined through her body and pooled at the very center of her being.

Just there, just waiting, until the moment he stiffened and surrendered to his need.

Her knees gave out, and he followed her down to the blanket.

"I'm not done with you yet," he murmured, levering himself onto his knees so she could move. "Look at me."

She rolled over and he covered her with his hot body, his hot erection, his heated mouth, his inexorable tongue.

"Did you think it was over?" he whispered, a breath above her lips. "Did you think I got nearly enough of you?" He pulled at her lower lip. "I'm *really* ready for you now." He claimed her mouth then, overpowering her, as hot and hard as the sun.

She felt the length of him flexing against her bare skin, and she gave up and went under, pulled by the relentless tide. He surrounded her, enfolded her; his body covered her, his legs entwining with hers, his merciless mouth demanding her complete surrender. She felt him testing her, insinuating those devastating fingers between her legs to feel her hot pliant flesh.

"Open yourself to me, Carrie. We're not done yet, you and I. Give yourself to me."

She made a low keening sound as she yielded herself

to him and he took her. "That's the way I want you. Just like that—" he explored her, touched her in the most intimate way possible "—unfurling like a flower..." He rolled over purposefully, bracing himself as he drove into her with one powerful thrust.

Carrie wrapped herself around him. She wanted every part of him covering her. She wanted his heat, his heart, his soul.

Truck rocketed against her, feeding hungrily on her mouth, engulfing her with his need to possess her. He burned for her, he felt as if they were Adam and Eve, as if he had waited a lifetime for her, as if he could sustain himself within her forever. But even he had his limits. He lost himself in her kisses, her body that met him thrust for thrust, and he lost it altogether as he swallowed her long low sexy growl as she reached completion, and pitched headlong into his own.

Then there was silence. A wafting breeze cooling their heated faces. The sounds of birds, cicadas, ducks, the low roar of a motorboat. Otherwise, not a movement, not a word. Just the sun, still burning hot, beating down on his nude body, heating him up again, and Carrie, naked in his arms, siren of his dreams.

"Carrie...?" He was kissing her swollen lips idly, playfully, nipping here, sucking there.

"Mmm?"

"I think we should go out on a date."

She barely heard him. She was drowsy with lust and satiation, and she didn't want him to move one inch. "Mmm."

"How about tonight?" He nuzzled her mouth, licking around the tender flesh inside her lips.

"Mmm...*what?*"

"Dinner."

"Where?"

"Out. With me."

Her forehead creased. "Like, going *out* out?"

"Like that. I just want to buy you dinner."

Dinner? Dinner out was a date, she thought. It meant people would see them together. People would assume things and make connections she didn't want them to make. Small towns were notorious for doing that.

"Not tonight."

"Why not? You have to eat dinner."

"I'm dieting."

Truck made a face and ran his hand down her sleek legs. "Try another excuse."

She struggled up onto her elbows. *Dear God, I am up on my roof, in broad daylight where anyone can see us. What is wrong with me?*

"Okay. How about we're not dating. We're having sex. And I don't want anyone to get the wrong idea."

"The *wrong* idea? And that would be what? You're hungry."

"We're a couple," she said succinctly, feeling distinctly uncomfortable now that she had defined the reality, at least as she saw it.

"Okay. We're not a couple. Let's grab a bite to eat."

"I'm not your bowling buddy either."

"You could be."

"Don't joke about this," she said sharply, struggling now to get away from his overwhelming presence. *Why did I do this, why did I leave myself open to this? Why does he have the power to do this to me?*

He levered himself upward immediately, and she looked up at him and felt every resolution dissolve into a swamping feeling of desire.

I can't fight this. Her throat got dry; she licked her lips.

The motion of her tongue arrested him. If she got on her knees, she would be at just the right height to taste him; she could own him with her mouth and hands. She was so beautiful, kneeling there. Truck watched her face, watched her response, edgy with the need to have her again. He wanted to feel her hands cup him, caress him, take him home.

Heat rose all around them. She swallowed hard. How could she let him go when he was practically begging her to feast on him?

The sexy lady embraces every facet of her sensuality and tries new things. She heard the words so clearly in her mind. Hadn't she written them?

Without missing a beat, she reached for him.

IF ONLY there didn't have to be the moments after, she thought, when the excitement died down and the heat dissipated. But how could you sustain that kind of high in the midst of sorting through your underwear and clothes and trying to get dressed without looking clumsy?

It never worked for her, even though Truck was unusually graceful at it. *Because he was so experienced?*

The sun was now down on the horizon. Truck was packing everything up and securing it with a tarp. Words seemed superfluous. Carrie climbed down from the roof first, hanging tight, not trusting her quivery legs.

She didn't wait for him either. She wanted to flee from him, and she wanted to run to him, and she hated those contradictory feelings.

"Carrie..."

She stopped and turned to face him, lured by that delicious little break in his voice.

Truck stood just by the ladder, his T-shirt slung over his shoulder, his fingers hooked into the waistband of his jeans, as dangerous as the devil, and twice as devious.

"Here's the deal," he said, his eyes glimmering with a positively wicked light. "Sex for dinner."

She froze. "I'll make sure I'm never hungry," she said tightly.

"And I'll make sure you're ravenous," he countered. "Today was just the appetizer. I haven't even begun to whet your appetite."

"I'll starve first." She knew exactly what he was doing.

He smiled that awful complacent *arrogant* male smile. "How long will that satisfy you? I think you'll be famished in a day, Carrie. I think you want it just as much as I do. So I guess we'll see who craves nourishment first."

He swirled his shirt off of his shoulders and yanked it over his head. "Me—I'm hungry. I'm going out to dinner." He flicked his hand at her. "See you, Carrie."

MEN! Fine. Truck had no conception of what she was going through, no idea about the choices she'd had to make. No clue what her life had been like before she'd come back to town or how much she'd given up. Just as well. A sexy lady could get a man like him out of her system in no time. And good sex didn't have to have anything to do with it.

Right. Or love.

On the other hand, after spending the afternoon in his arms, her bed seemed awfully cold and lonely. But Carrie didn't like the alternatives either: ignore him—*impossible*—or get involved with him—*impossible*.

The next awful step was to suggest they could be friends.

Actually I thought we were in love...

Heat washed her face as she remembered his words. What did he think they were *in* now?

Heat. Sex. And she'd desperately wanted him, so what did that do to all her fuzzy logic about involvement?

This *was* involvement.

Okay, I won't fight it. I'll be involved. I just won't go out to dinner. I'll do the sexy lady bit: How could any man resist?

HE MIGHT AS WELL be a thousand miles away as just up the road from her, Truck thought as he maneuvered his car into the garage at the back of the house. She wasn't going to let him any closer than he'd gotten already.

God, Carrie was something. Now he knew why he had waited, why no other woman had ever done it for him, why he'd come back to Paradise. He didn't believe it was fate. He was beginning to think it was inevitable.

The problem was, he still had to capture the castle. And his warrior princess had pulled up the bridge across the moat. She was not making it easy. Oh, she was worth it. Truck was still wrung out from this afternoon, and he already craved more. He was not going to let her just walk away either. Not this time. Not ever.

He dropped onto one of the chairs on the enclosed porch and stared out across the road at the pond. There wasn't much to see at this hour: just the clear, star-studded sky, the looming trees across the road, the flick of a lightning bug. And it was quiet, except for the crickets, the faint honk of a duck, a distant engine as a car raced up the Pond Road.

Truck liked the quiet, the peace, the sense of space and containment both. He liked working with his hands and caring for Old Man. He liked the town, the people, the life he'd chosen far from the fast lanes of Chicago where he'd first started out.

Where he'd almost been devoured by his resentment of Carrie's rejection and his suppressed feelings of abandonment; where he'd become utterly self-destructive and out of control.

The career had gone first—his abortive desire to be a journalist. You couldn't cover a beat when you weren't sober. And half the time he hadn't been.

He hadn't been much different than Carrie, he thought. He couldn't count how many women he'd had, how many meaningless encounters, how many nights he'd spent in someone's bed whose name he couldn't remember the next morning, women he eliminated from his life without a shred of remorse, women from whom he'd run away.

A man found his soul in the strangest places.

In the bathroom of a plane, throwing up his guts, on the way home to deal with his father's tragic accident. In a hospital room, praying for Old Man to live. In the kindness of strangers who transferred their affection for Old Man onto his worthless only child and forced him to become a man.

In the depths of the pond on a quiet autumn day as he paddled a canoe out to the center and watched the sun go down. In the heft of a tool precision-crafted to do precisely the job you needed it to do. In the joy of fitting the pieces of a puzzle together and making it whole, whether it was plumbing, making love or your life.

This he had learned sometime somewhere in his twenty-seventh year, when he returned to Paradise to take over the business and take care of Old Man.

Truck heard the unmistakable sound of Old Man's wheelchair rolling across the living-room floor.

"You out there?"

"Yep."

Old Man appeared on the threshold. "So, you finished up in Searsport?"

"Yep." Truck knew that wasn't what Old Man wanted to know.

"Been working down at Carrie's then?"

Bingo. "Uh-huh."

"How's she doing?"

"She's fighting every inch of the way."

"It's hard to keep 'em down on the farm, that's for sure. There's nothing like the pull of the big bad city. You think she'll leave eventually?" Old Man asked idly.

"She thinks she will."

"Too bad."

"Things change," Truck said softly.

"Change is hard," Old Man said.

"We all change," he said to Old Man.

"One way or another," Old Man agreed. "Bring Carrie up to dinner sometime soon. I'll tell Jolley."

"I'll do that," Truck said.

Old Man reached out and touched his arm. "Good night, son."

Truck squeezed his hand. "'Night." He listened to the wheels in the darkness as Old Man returned to his room. He felt the knife edge of desire cut into him, but he *wanted* to feel the tormenting ache, the desire. It was his secret, his insatiable hunger for Carrie, and it was his to revel in. He felt the heat, the thickness of the night air. More than anything he wanted to climb in Carrie's bedroom window right this very second. She'd wake up, she'd want him and she'd take him, and then she'd let him ride her hard.

Fantasies and dreams—

...Actually, I thought it was love...

IT WAS HOT, it was late, and Carrie was wide awake, her body covered with a sheen of perspiration.

This isn't fair. I don't want to think about him. I don't want him, I don't...

I do. If he came in that window right now—if...stupid fantasy...if—I would...

She drew in a hissing breath. She had never felt so voluptuous. That was the thing that awakened her, her body swelling and stretching with this intense yearning, priming her, making her wet, hot and ready before she was even aware of her need.

Ready for what? Fantasies and dreams?

He could have been with her now. He could have stayed the whole night right in this bed.

If she knew magic, she'd conjure him up in a heartbeat, naked and throbbing, and blinded by his overwhelming need for her body.

What was he thinking? What was he doing? Why didn't he come?

Dangerous feelings. Shameless desires, especially for one as determined as she was not to have a relationship, not to make a home here.

It was crazy to want him. Insane not to consider the ramifications.

Wasn't it enough she had spent that glorious afternoon with him on the roof, for heaven's sake?

She didn't want to answer that question.

It wasn't enough. She shook herself. The truth was, living in Paradise was making her stir-crazy. She had too much time on her hands and too much libido.

She wished he would come...

She awakened again hours later, joltingly aware that there was someone else in the room, and that for some reason her arms were immobile.

She pulled against the restraints, twisting and bucking her body, fear coursing through her. Then her eyes became accustomed to the dark, and she saw him, standing at the foot of the bed, watching, and she stopped her writhing as he waited, looking dark, sensual, hungry, driven to the edge...

Yes... Her breath caught as she pulled at the restraints, feeling the soft stretch of the material, and the dawning comprehension that she was fully in control. *Yes.*

Her excitement grew. He wanted her. He couldn't help himself. He was over the edge...

He wore nothing under his jeans but his rampaging desire for her. He climbed onto the bed, his naked need joining with hers.

"I'm hard for you." His voice was barely above a breath. His body was slick with sweat, burningly aroused.

She made that helpless little sound as he rocked against her.

"Is this what you want, Carrie?" He pushed deeper and she gasped. "And this?" He pulled this time, a long lingering stroke outward. "You want what I have?"

Her body liquefied, expanded, took him deeper as he braced himself above her at just the angle to watch her undulations and her pleasure.

He pushed farther, rotating his hips, squeezing himself tighter and tighter against her so she felt the unmistakable mating of their bodies.

"Don't move." Did he say it? Did she?

She was so open to him, so connected; she couldn't conceive of another reality but this sensual joining in the dark.

He was positioned at her very center, the rock on which she rooted. He didn't have to move; she took him, bearing down on him, writhing back and forth, against him.

And the thing that made it even more exciting was the binding of her hands so that the movement of her body defined her pleasure; and the way he lay canted over her, watching her, moving with her in short, little strokes so she could just feel his pumping hips.

Just right. Just...right—as she bore down on the rhythmic thrusts. Just right...how did he know—of course he knew...her breath came faster as the tension built, as sensation piled on sensation like whipped cream on cake, and just a firm swipe of the tongue would do it—there...and *there*; her body quickened, she held suspended for one fraught moment and then she let go.

He caught her, driving into the waves of her climax, pulling it from her and pulling it from her until she begged for mercy, until he could pull no more and the only thing left was to give himself up to her desire.

OR HAD SHE DREAMED *the whole thing?*

When she awakened the next morning, she was alone. No Truck. No bonds. No sign that anyone had been in the house. Had been in her bed.

And only the expansive sense of well-being she felt told her that maybe, just maybe, fantasies did come true...

7

SUNDAYS IN PARADISE consisted of going to church in the morning, visiting family and friends in the afternoon, and in the spring and summer browsing through the local flea market and garage sales.

The big Segers outdoor flea market was a seasonal event that ran from May through October on four acres of undeveloped land about a half mile out of town. Since anyone could set up a table for two dollars a shot, the flea market was an amiable mix of people cleaning out attics and garages; dealers of coins, cards, comics; collectors looking for a profit; and dealers looking to get rid of slow-selling items.

You could find clothes, used paperbacks, baby items, cookware, records and CDs, tools, furniture, dishes and sometimes even an ancient car.

It was one of Jeannie's favorite places to come on a Sunday after church, and she roused up Carrie with promises of treasure and sun and fun.

"I'd rather go to the lake," Carrie grumbled.

"You can do that too. Come on. I bet you haven't even had breakfast yet."

"Just barely."

"And I suppose you wouldn't call yourself dressed."

"Not hardly."

"Shoot. You know you have to get there early to get the best stuff."

"I'm not looking for stuff," Carrie said.

"You will be," Jeannie said confidently.

Jeannie was at Carrie's within an hour. As Carrie dressed, Jeannie waited for her in the living room.

Carrie was having trouble coming to grips with Jeannie's new sexy-lady image. The whole time she was dressing, Carrie was debating whether she should say something to Jeannie about the fact that perhaps she was overplaying the sexy-lady thing. Jeannie wore one of the new bodysuits with a sweetheart neckline that displayed her cleavage, one of the long button-front skirts, unbuttoned almost to her thighs, new sandals, new jewelry, and her hair was swept up off her neck. On top of all that, she had on makeup that emphasized her eyes and mouth, a bolder look that so disconcerted Carrie, she finally decided to say something...at least just about the makeup.

"Oh this? I went to Portland the other afternoon, and fell for the line at the makeup counter at Lorstan's. I think it looks pretty good."

"Pretty different."

"You're not so bad yourself," Jeannie said, eyeing Carrie's black jeans and tiger-print tank top. "And it's not as if you don't load up on eyeliner and lipstick yourself."

"That's true," Carrie acknowledged. "It just takes some getting used to on you."

"That's what Eddie said."

"Oh—Eddie—" Carrie motioned her out the door. "How is Eddie taking all this?"

"He doesn't understand it, and he doesn't like it."

"Because—?"

"He doesn't understand it. And I say—*good.*"

Carrie thought it best to leave the subject alone for now, and changed the topic.

"You know," Carrie said as she opened the car door, "I keep thinking you dream up these little side trips to prevent me from zooming around town on my cycle."

"You're right," Jeannie said. "When you're right, you're right. But—if you ever went to a flea market and found the perfect, oh, lamp, how would you get it home?"

"I'd call on my friends, of course," Carrie said lightly as Jeannie backed the car up the track and turned onto the road.

"So how's Truck doing?" Jeannie asked casually after a few minutes.

Carrie's heart started pounding. She wondered if Jeannie knew anything, if Jeannie could have seen anything from her house. Oh damn. It was probably the most innocent question. Still, if such an innocent question could make her feel so guilty, it was yet another reason not to let herself get much more entangled with Truck.

Oh? Much more? She kept pushing down the rising desire she felt every time she thought about last night—assuming she hadn't dreamed last night...

"Truck?" Her voice sounded normal, if a little high. "He's doing fine, I guess. He was away last week, did you know?"

"Yep, I did. Story about it in the paper. They pulled in a dozen companies from all over the state to salvage that pipeline."

So what did you mean by that question, Jeannie?

They were rolling through the main street of Segers, past the bank and post office, the auto store, and the radio station. Jeannie turned left, and immediately they came upon a line of cars that stretched up the road.

"Whoa. A lot of people today. We might just as well try to park where we can and walk over."

The field was covered with vendors' tables and people wandering around. Jeannie, it turned out, was an avid collector of kitchen accessories from the fifties, and she was off and running the minute they got to the edge of the field.

Carrie drifted up and down the aisles, looking at books, crafts, a booth selling old jeans. *Old jeans! She who used to shop in designer stores for casual clothes...looking at used jeans?*

Well, it was time to learn to be frugal, she thought as she bought a pair of worn bleached-out jeans that were as soft as a baby blanket. She bought some paperback novels, and a large shallow bowl because she liked its shape.

"That's beginning to look a little permanent."

Carrie wheeled around, her heart pounding.

Truck. Right over her shoulder. Looming. Luscious. No man had a right to look that good this early in the afternoon. He was dressed all in blue today, wearing a cotton shirt tucked into his jeans with the sleeves rolled up to his elbows.

"What are you doing here?" she asked, cursing the tremble in her voice.

"Meeting and greeting the neighbors. And I collect old tools. I don't expect you knew that."

"No." Carrie noticed that other women, old and young, were also looking at him, and why not? He was so magnetic, he radiated such a sensual aura she almost couldn't stand it. Her mind suddenly went blank and she couldn't think of a thing to say to Truck. Nothing that would keep him by her side or that would give her any clue as to whether she might see him later.

The vendor handed her the bag with her bowl. Carrie shoved the books and jeans on top of it, frantically searching for something to say.

"I came with Jeannie," she blurted out after a long silence.

Truck's eyes darkened, but he couldn't think of a comeback that wouldn't cause the three old ladies beside them to have a heart attack. Carrie looked good enough to eat, and that formfitting top and jeans she wore only fired up his imagination all over again, but all he said was, "Yeah, what is with Jeannie? She's wearing skirts these days. And makeup. I don't know how radical that is, but she looks a damn sight prettier and sexier."

"She does, doesn't she? Think Eddie cares?"

Truck hesitated a minute. Everyone knew Eddie didn't care. "No," he said finally.

"Think Tom does?" Carrie asked, motioning toward where Jeannie stood talking to him. Tom looked as if he was positively hanging on Jeannie's every word. And she was doing that intense eye contact, and listening. All the things that came under the banner of the tricks of the sexy lady—tricks that might lose her husband.

"Yeah, I do. But that's Jeannie's problem."

Maybe not. Maybe it's mine, because I let it go too far...

Truck touched her arm, startling her. "I have to go get Old Man."

"Okay." It wasn't. She wanted him to stay. No, to take her home and do all the things with her he had done last night. She watched him stride away, a man with purpose who loved his father and was content with his life.

Everyone knew him and called out greetings, and he

stopped to talk to one or the other of them as he made his way from the field to his car. He could have seen them all yesterday, Carrie thought, and he was just as happy to see them today.

"Oh, I didn't get a chance to talk to Trucker," Jeannie said, coming up beside her. "Everything okay? Old Man?"

"He was just going to pick him up from somewhere. What about you?" Carrie asked quickly, not wanting to talk about Truck with Jeannie.

"Oh, I have a load of stuff—Tom's watching it for me. C'mon, he'll help us load up. What'd you come up with?"

"Books, a bowl, some jeans."

"Hey," Jeannie said with a grin, "some haul for someone who wasn't in a buying mood."

"It's fun," Carrie said. "I wouldn't mind coming again."

They got everything back to the car in due course, stopping along the way so Jeannie could chat with friends. She looked so happy, so confident that Carrie was just a little scared.

Uplift didn't work in quite that way, quite that fast, she didn't think. But certainly Tom was aware of it, of Jeannie's body and her smile, her thick hair shining in the sun, and her focus on him.

"You really got those sexy-lady lessons down," Carrie commented as they drove home.

"They work," Jeannie said. "Maybe not on everyone. But they work."

Carrie hesitated. She wanted to say something, she wasn't sure she should. Finally, she murmured, "Be careful. You might be playing with fire."

"Well, guess what, Carrie," Jeannie said, and there

was no acrimony in her tone. "Maybe it's nice to feel hot for a change."

Carrie's heart sank. If something happened between Jeannie and Eddie, if they separated, or Jeannie left him, she would know the reason why...and Carrie would be the one responsible.

THE HOUSE WAS STARTING to look habitable. Now that things had aired out, and she'd replaced some of the sheets and towels and bought new blankets, pillows and a wonderful old bowl, the house seemed warmer, more inviting, but so very quiet...and lonely.

People visited family on Sunday and went out to dinner with friends. She remembered that from before; she and her mother had no family, and all her mother's friends had other obligations, so they'd usually spent Sundays together, making dinner, listening to music.

Sundays had been particularly hard on her mother. Her mother had been too lonely too long, Sundays had always brought it home.

Carrie placed the bowl on the coffee table, and the stack of paperbacks beside it. She could read tonight or listen to the radio. She didn't miss having a TV, and that shocked her a little. Instead she was spending the time on-line, searching job banks and networking across the country. Not that it had yielded anything yet. Still, she'd only been out of circulation a little more than two weeks.

Two weeks! Only two weeks, and already her life had been turned inside out all over again.

She could not let her desire for Truck get in the way of anything else.

Easier said, she thought, curling up on the couch. It wasn't as if there were some on-off switch. It was more like she was stuck on permanent burn.

And then last night—*oh, last night*...

...Is this what you want? And this...?

She felt herself heating up. *This*...

She jumped up from the couch. She had to stop thinking about him. She needed a cold shower...*and a hot man*—

She drew in a sharp breath. Lord, Truck had her coming and going.

Enough of that...

...Did you think I got enough of you...?

Did she ever think that her feelings for him were just lying dormant and that they would blaze up into this all-consuming conflagration?

No. No. That was the trap. That was the bait. You got so sexually entangled with a man that you got tied up in marriage and motherhood, and so constricted and constrained that there was no room for anything else.

And then fifteen years later, you woke up, like Jeannie, and discovered you weren't living the life you thought you were.

Dear God, how must Jeannie have felt when Carrie had come back to town, fresh off of a glamorous life in New York?

Suddenly Carrie felt a burst of frustration like she'd done nothing right since she came back to town. And for someone who didn't want to stay, she was getting awfully involved with Jeannie and Truck. Well, that would end soon. Something would turn up. And what was happening with Truck was just a side issue. There was no question. Career came first. But still...after yesterday, didn't she feel sometimes, truly, she would give it all up...for Truck?

She groaned. Maybe, in her deepest heart, she was trying to find a way to have everything she wanted, even though she knew it wasn't possible.

And anyway, love didn't last. Look at Jeannie and

PLAY TIC-TAC-TOE

OR FREE BOOKS AND A GREAT FREE GIFT!

Use this sticker to **PLAY TIC-TAC-TOE**. See instructions inside!

THERE'S NO COST*NO OBLIGATION!

Get **2** books and a fabulous mystery gift! **ABSOLUTELY FREE!**

Turn the page to play!

Play TIC-TAC-TOE and get FREE GIFTS!

HOW TO PLAY:

1. Play the tic-tac-toe scratch-off game at the right for your FREE BOOKS and FREE GIFT!

2. Send back this card and you'll receive TWO brand-new Harlequin Temptation® novels. These books have a cover price of $3.75 each in the U.S. and $4.25 each in Canada, but they are yours to keep absolutely free.

3. There's no catch. You're under no obligation to buy anything. We charge nothing — ZERO — for your first shipment. And you don't have to make any minimum number of purchases — not even one!

4. The fact is, thousands of readers enjoy receiving books by mail from the Harlequin Reader Service® months before they're available in stores. They like the convenience of home delivery, and they love our discount prices!

5. We hope that after receiving your free books you'll want to remain a subscriber. But the choice is yours — to continue or cancel, any time at all! So why not take us up on our invitation, with no risk of any kind. You'll be glad you did!

YOURS FREE
A FABULOUS MYSTERY GIFT!

**We can't tell you what it is…
but we're sure you'll like it!**

A FREE GIFT –
just for playing
TIC-TAC-TOE!

DETACH AND MAIL CARD TODAY!

With a coin, scratch the gold boxes on the tic-tac-toe board. Then remove the "X" sticker from the front and affix it so that you get three X's in a row. This means you can get **TWO FREE** Harlequin Temptation® novels and a **FREE MYSTERY GIFT!**

PLAY TIC-TAC-TOE

YES! Please send me the 2 Free books and gift for which I qualify. I understand that I am under no obligation to purchase any books, as explained on the back of this card.

342 HDL CX7H

142 HDL CX66
(H-T-12/99)

Name:	
	(PLEASE PRINT CLEARLY)
Address:	Apt.#:
City:	State/Prov.:	Zip/Postal Code:

Offer limited to one per household and not valid to current Harlequin Temptation® subscribers. All orders subject to approval.

PRINTED IN U.S.A

The Harlequin Reader Service® — Here's how it works:

Accepting your 2 free books and gift places you under no obligation to buy anything. You may keep the books and gift and return the shipping statement marked "cancel." If you do not cancel, about a month later we'll send you 4 additional novels and bill you just $3.12 each in the U.S., or $3.57 each in Canada, plus 25¢ delivery per book and applicable taxes if any.* That's the complete price and — compared to the cover price of $3.75 in the U.S. and $4.25 in Canada — it's quite a bargain! You may cancel at any time, but if you choose to continue, every month we'll send you 4 more books, which you may either purchase at the discount price or return to us and cancel your subscription.

*Terms and prices subject to change without notice. Sales tax applicable in N.Y. Canadian residents will be charged applicable provincial taxes and GST.

Eddie. But a career went on forever. It was just a matter of footwork and timing. And perseverence.

The call would come and she knew she wouldn't hesitate. Career came first. She would be out of here...soon.

THERE WAS ONLY one way to handle Carrie, Truck decided, and that was to give her what she wanted—with a catch. And especially since she was so dead set on thinking that her stay in Paradise was only temporary. Some things weren't temporary, like his fierce desire for Carrie every time he thought about her, every time he saw her.

This afternoon had been rough. There'd been too many people around and he'd wound up making banal conversation while he'd been feeling as primitive as a caveman and out of control.

"So, did you ask Carrie to dinner?" Old Man asked him when Truck had got him back home.

"Carrie isn't doing dinner with the locals," he answered.

Old Man cocked his head. "Is that so?"

"That is most definitely so," he said, lightening his tone.

"That's too bad." There was a long pause. "Have you ever asked her?"

Longer pause. "Kind of," Truck said finally.

Short pause. "I see," Old Man said.

The problem was, his father saw too much, Truck thought. His father probably knew just how Truck felt about Carrie. And exactly what he meant by *kind of*. Nothing got by Old Man.

Truck sat on the porch and waited for Old Man to fall asleep. He then wheeled his father into his bedroom, gently lifted him out of the wheelchair and put him to bed. Afterward he went back outside and waited some more. He had learned the value of patience and anticipation. He reined in his imagination. There was plenty of time for that later. For now, he had to take control. Carrie was not going to be allowed to deny what was going on between them.

It had gone too far for that anyway.

Carrie was working intently on her computer when late that night he let himself into her house. Lights were blazing everywhere, and he turned them down as he entered the kitchen, went through the living room and paused at the door to the den.

She still wasn't aware of him. He watched her for a moment, his whole body tensing. He flicked off the overhead light so that only the muted glow of the desk lamp lit the room.

She jumped and pushed backward on her desk chair. "Who's there?"

"Just me."

She ran her tongue over her lips; the movement arrested him. "It's after midnight."

"I know." He pushed her chair back to the desk and the flickering screen.

"What are you doing here?"

He placed his hands on her shoulders and he felt the shuddering excitement building in her. She understood why he was here, he would not have to play games.

He slipped his hands downward to the swell of her breasts and cupped them. All her secrets right here in this one motion of his hands sliding under and around the curve of her breasts, his fingers swirling over and around them, but never touching her nipples.

"You know what I'm doing here." He could feel her body caving right under his hands. "I'm your phantom lover, Carrie. I come in the night to lie with you, so you never have to be seen with me, you never have to talk to me, you never have to make a commitment to me."

He deliberately intensified the swirling motion, coming closer and closer to her hard-peaked nipples. "Is that how you want it, Carrie? In the dark, deep of the night, when prying eyes can't see?"

She arched her breasts into his hands. Her whole body went weak with a swooning excitement. He could do anything with her he wanted. She felt like clay, soft, pliant, rich.

"I want *you*," she whispered, in thrall to his long fingers stroking her breasts.

Truck cupped her breasts again and urged her out of her chair. "Make yourself ready for me." No niceties here, but she didn't need that, only the insistent caress of his fingers all over her breasts, and permission to give in to her burning need. "Over the desk."

He would show her that he was more than a memory, more than a phantom lover that came to her at night, and then, only then would Carrie keep him with her forever.

It was just the right height, and her bottom was canted at exactly the right angle. He kneaded the cushiony curves of her buttocks as he ripped off his jeans. She wanted this as much as he.

Her shuddering breaths aroused him still more. Slowly he pushed himself into her, letting her feel his power, his heat.

Carrie could feel only the length and thickness of him, and his huge wicked hands holding her body immobile to receive him. She shimmied against his hips in flagrant anticipation, and he whispered in a husky tone, "Not yet. Don't move. I want more of you."

How much more? She caught her breath. *That much more.* She groaned, she threw her head back, moaned loudly as she felt him wholly rooted in her.

Silence. Heat. Swelling tension. Explosive need. Not a movement, not a word. Everything understood by their hot voluptuous joining.

And he waited. He understood so well the virtue of anticipation, of letting her experience the hard thick whole of his maleness inside her, and nurturing her appetite for it. It was enough for now that she wanted him right this minute in the worst way.

And that was how he intended to keep her: aroused and hungry and primed for him. It was almost time…he felt it, he heard it in the soft sounds she made at the back of her throat. He grasped her hips, he shifted his stance, and he poised himself for the wild drive to completion. He heard her keening cry as he initiated a short rhythmic thrust that removed him from the depths of her. Again he slowed himself, pulling out and pushing in tirelessly, rhythmically, until she melted around him, begging him for more.

Then he took her, giving in to his volcanic craving for her.

Silence again. There were no words. Carrie lay sprawled across the desk, utterly spent and weak.

She thought he had left her to go to the kitchen. Or maybe he was sitting on the porch. But when she finally dressed herself, shut down the computer and went to look for him, he was nowhere in the house, and she felt a little lost.

…Did you think I got nearly enough of you…?

Her phantom lover…

A smile played around her lips. *He sure was playing it to the hilt.*

And here was the good part, she thought. *For as long as she remained in Paradise, she could have him and her freedom too.*

CARRIE WAS JUST NOT USED to not working. There was something about having a daily routine that made it easier to get things done, and after these initial two weeks, she was feeling a little discomfitted.

Not that she didn't have things to do. Today there was laundry, for one thing, and she needed to check the post-office box she'd rented. She had some proposals and drawings she needed scanned at the local office-supply store. She needed groceries. And a couple of things at the discount store.

It was just not the kind of thing she was used to doing.

She still hadn't come to terms with it—the fact she wasn't racing out the door every morning to go to work or to meet some deadline.

And then, she was worried about Jeannie. And what to do about Truck.

But maybe she didn't need to do anything about Truck. He was doing it all himself, and she couldn't argue with the consequences. *A phantom lover...her phantom lover.* Her body twinged at just the thought of it. She dressed in anticipation of it, though. She didn't expect to run into him at the post office.

"Hey, Carrie." Neutral tone. Nothing in his expression. Lethal looks today, long and lean in black, his hair uncombed, his expression uncomfortably indifferent.

"Truck." What did she expect? "Come here often?"

"Bills are going out today. What about you?"

Had he really been her phantom lover last night? "I'm just getting my mail. I rented a box."

Was she looking a little uneasy that he didn't acknowledge their explosive coupling last night? Good, he thought. And this was just the first step. "I won't keep you then," he said.

Keep me...! Carrie couldn't believe how noncommittal he was. "See you." She turned to the bank of rental boxes and never saw his glimmering smile. Only saw the handful of letters that meant she had been considered and rejected yet again.

Ah well...

She stopped at Bob Verity's store to pick up her papers which she now had on reserve.

"So how's Truck coming with your house?" Bob asked.

"I can flush the toilet and take a shower. That's about all I need right now," Carrie said, her tone terse. She had to watch that. Bob lived on the other side of the pond. She wondered if he'd seen her and Truck on the roof all those days ago.

Damn it, damn it. No one could've seen anything through those trees unless they were flying low at five hundred feet.

Well, she couldn't undo that, not now. She had to act natural, normal, and just slough it off.

Next she was on to the bank to make a withdrawal and chat with Jeannie. She looked phenomenal today, dressed in one of her old suits, but with the added dash of a new bodysuit, the look-at-me jewelry, the makeup.

"Well, don't you look terrific," Carrie complimented her.

"Don't you." Jeannie smiled. "There's something about you and those gold colors. Kind of primitive and dangerous. You feeling like that today, oh mighty huntress?"

"I'm feeling more like roadkill," Carrie said ruefully.

"I got some more don't-call-us-we'll-call-you letters. So it's back to the drawing board."

"Well, then, you work hard all week and you'll have the Bean-Hole Bean Festival to look forward to this weekend."

"Sure," Carrie murmured distractedly, counting the thin stack of bills Jeannie had handed her.

"I'll call for you Saturday morning."

"Same time, same place?" Carrie asked.

"Something like that," Jeannie said, so offhandedly that Carrie pricked up.

"See you then," she said, wondering if Jeannie weren't using her somehow—as cover? To see Tom in a public place? *Oh, Jeannie...*

The office-supply store was next on her list, and then it was over to the discount store for some brooms and vacuum-cleaner bags. After she shopped and put everything away, she didn't feel like doing anything much more than sitting on the porch.

It was time for a reality check. She had to seriously consider trying to find a job in Portland. Portland was about forty minutes down the turnpike in good weather. But she'd have to get a car, and maybe a snowplow. She'd have to get the house rewired and winterized, buy sheepskin boots, down coats and comforters, and lay in wood...

But she'd have Truck, she thought. If she decided not to go, if she found work, for as long as she wanted him, she would have Truck. And that was almost enough to make her stay.

8

OF COURSE that was assuming her *phantom lover* still wanted her. As the week went on, Carrie wasn't so sure. And it wasn't a situation where she could call Truck and ask him outright. But the not knowing was horrible, and the anticipation unbearable. She wondered what it was doing to him. Probably nothing, if he could look her in the eye and act so casually.

Men...

The nights were the worst, when she restlessly tossed and turned, listening for his footsteps, craving his touch.

This could get very out of hand.

I won't let it.

I have better things to do than pine for him.

Having made that resolution, Carrie began looking around town with new eyes, determined that since she might be staying in Paradise, she'd better start making the best of it. If there wasn't a job out there for her, then maybe it was time to create one for herself.

Paradise and the surrounding towns could really benefit from an influx of new residents and vacationers. Maybe Carrie could come up with an ad campaign to attract new vacationers—and maybe even new businesses—to the area just the way Paradise's chamber of commerce had gone after young professionals.

It felt good to be able to take action, even if the payoff would be way in the future. And to push aside all thoughts of Truck. And to make some contacts, athough she hadn't made a cold call in years.

Carrie started at the chamber of commerce with Peter Stoddard, whom she'd met in passing at the Grange Hall dance. He was a lawyer who had decided that quality of life was worth far more than the partner track at some prestigious law firm. And he meant to make the most of being a fairly big fish in a small pond.

"I like affecting change from the ground up," he told Carrie as he greeted her in his office on Main Street. He had a small conversational area set up in one corner, and he gestured for her to take a seat in one of the two leather wing chairs. "It could lead to bigger things."

She could see it clearly—Peter was the kind of man who would get involved, who believed in civic participation, and that kind of dedication might well lead right to municipal and ultimately state politics.

"So what can I do for you?" Peter asked.

"I'd like to help the chamber bring more tourists and business investments to the area."

Carrie felt his interest prick up immediately.

"I always like to hear about generating dollars in town. How?"

Here came the tricky part. "Advertising and promotion."

"No money for that, Carrie. You know that."

"The chamber got you here through advertising and promotion," Carrie pointed out. "I think if the trilake chambers of commerce pooled their resources, they could afford to take on an experienced freelance advertising director who would handle all aspects of the promotion, from art and copy to timing and placement in the proper media, and that would include outside the state too."

Peter thought about it a moment. "Okay. And this advertising director would be...?"

"Me. I have fifteen years' experience in all areas, on all levels with all manner of clients. I'll leave you a résumé. But what I want you to think about is that this little corner of Maine is one of the best-kept secrets around. It's rural, but not even an hour from Portland, and within driving distance of Boston. You have summer and winter sports, theater, concerts, museums, university and community functions, an arts community, and on top of that, you have inexpensive housing, decent schools and an employment base that's second to none.

"There's an incredible opportunity here for new businesses to come in for no money at all, obtain a willing workforce and all the quality of life that brought you and Tom and others here in the first place. And that was just from some ads in the Portland papers."

Carrie leaned forward as she saw it all clearly in her mind: what they had to do, where they had to go.

"What if you went farther afield?" she said. "What if you prepared a magazine supplement and got the campaign into every Sunday paper across the country? What if you did a selective mailing to businesses you knew were looking to relocate? What if you contacted everyone who'd gone to camp up here with a promotional piece about the Paradise they knew and loved? What if—"

"Whoa," Peter held up his hands. "Slow down."

Carrie sat back. "It's such a great idea! We could get the radio station involved, and the newspaper—and then create a Web site—"

Peter was shaking his head and laughing. "Okay."

"What?" She stopped short. She did like a decisive man.

"I said okay. You caught us at the right time. We had some meetings on attracting new businesses just last week. So, write up a proposal. Detail everything, including media expenses, and what you reasonably expect to charge for creating and supervising this campaign. You'll have to do it on a dime, Carrie, if you expect the chamber to approve it. They're serious about improving the economy, so this can't be some New York pie-in-the-sky campaign."

"I'm a native of Paradise, I know every good thing about it," she said confidently, then wondered at her certainty. Rather, she knew everything about it from the point of view of a salesperson, not from her heart.

But maybe her heart was beginning to enter into it, she thought after she'd left the meeting with Peter optimistic about her proposal for the first time since she'd come home.

Home...well, well, well—she was thinking of it as home...

Carrie stopped in town to pick up some groceries at Verity's store, and as she was backing out on her motorcycle she saw a sign in the hardware-store window:

Help Wanted. Part-time.

Carrie shut down the engine and sat there, biting her lip. No. Yes. She wasn't desperate yet, but her bank balance was diminishing daily, and whatever happened with Peter and the promotion piece, she wouldn't see any money from it for months. And taxes were upcoming, and payment due to Truck for services rendered—

Oh dear God, can I not stop thinking about Truck?

How bad could it be? Hourly wage. In town. Part-time, so she'd be able to continue working on the project she'd initiated today—if it worked out. Immediate money, and at this point, anything was better than nothing. All good reasons for walking into that store and asking for the job, whatever it was.

Carrie knew how to do that. Sometimes you had to seize the moment, just as she had done with Peter Stoddard not a half hour ago.

"Can I help you?" A gangly teenager met her as she walked in the door of the hardware store.

"Um, the sign in the window," Carrie said. "I'm interested in the job. Is there someone I could speak to?"

"Yeah...Mr. Longford." He turned and shouted, "Mr. Longford, Mr. Longford," and a moment later a tall older man came out of the back of the store and motioned her over.

She held out her hand. "I'm Carrie Spencer," she said, clasping his. "I live over on the Pond."

"Sure, sure. I knew your mother, come on in, sit down."

She followed him to a tiny office in the ell of the antique building that housed the store. His desk was crammed with papers, order forms, a computer and printer, and there were file cabinets spilling over, and shelves piled with catalogs.

Suddenly she had second thoughts. What if the call came? What if someone wanted her tomorrow in Boston or Los Angeles?

Fool. She took a deep breath. "I saw the sign outside. I need an interim position right now, but I honestly couldn't guarantee I wouldn't have to leave tomorrow. So maybe this isn't a good idea..."

"No, no. Sit. Want some coffee? No? Okay. Well, I've been advertising in the papers about a month, and I haven't had any qualified candidates apply for this job. Mainly high-school seniors, but this isn't stuff I'd entrust to them, even with courses in business under their belts.

I'm looking for someone to do the ordering, the book-keeping, and generally make sense out of a system I've allowed to become very sloppy."

He sent her a rueful smile. "So-o-o, let's see if we can help each other. The way I understand it, you've been downsized and you've been looking for a similar position, but you haven't yet had much luck."

Carrie blinked, shocked that he knew so much about her. "How do you know that?"

"Everybody knows."

The scariest words in the English language, she thought.

"So," Mr. Longford continued, "let me propose you come in and start ordering the chaos for, oh, seven dollars an hour, mornings, eight to noon every day, that is, if you have the experience to handle it, and if something comes through for you, well, we'll talk about it then."

"I was a secretary for a lot of years," Carrie said. "I can handle it."

"Good. I'd like to hire you. My wife handles payroll. You come in tomorrow first thing, and we'll get started."

Simple as that. Straightforward, to the point, no convoluted paperwork and interviews.

Carrie stopped off at the bank and told Jeannie.

"Oh good," Jeannie said. "We can do lunch."

"I'll have my calculator call yours," Carrie said, waving at her. "See you."

She couldn't believe how much better she felt, knowing she had a place to go and something to do.

And then she had the wind knocked out of her when she finally got back to the house. Truck had been there, working in the crawlspace and the bathroom, but he was gone. He hadn't waited for her to come home.

Sometimes it was better to be elusive.

That wasn't usually the male position, Truck thought, but he wanted to keep Carrie off guard and ravenous—for him...like he was for her. He burned for her all day long, tortured by his memories and fantasies of what he would do once they were together.

Truck didn't know how he had stayed away from her for three days. He should have stayed this afternoon, should have waited for her, but there was time enough tonight. There would be Carrie in her bed, yearning for the phantom lover who would take her in the dark—there was a fantasy to nourish a man's desire.

Him. Soon. *Loving* her. And calling it something else altogether.

Truck eased his way into her house toward midnight, not quite knowing what to expect. The living room was dark as was the den. But the light was on in the kitchen, and Carrie sat at the counter, papers strewn all around her, sketching away, tensing as she heard his step.

He paused on the threshold and watched as she composed herself before she met his gaze.

"I hope you didn't feel you *had* to come," Carrie said finally, as if she hadn't been sitting there and yearning for him.

"I hope you didn't feel you had to say that," he countered, matching her tone. "This is what *you* want. A hot body in the dark and no contact during the day. I'm here. I'm willing—tonight, and any night—so when you're in the mood—"

He didn't finish the sentence and she looked up sharply.

"—just whistle."

He was on the last porch step when he heard her,

damn her for waiting so long. It was one thing to call a bluff. It was another for her to torture him with it.

Truck took his time reentering the house, sloughing off his shirt, his boots, his socks on the way, and unzipping his jeans right to his root, before he got to the kitchen door.

Her throat had gone dry when he appeared in the doorway, his jeans slung low on his hips and unzipped down to there to tantalize her. He was naked under his jeans, his rigid manhood bulging tight. She felt herself quickening, becoming liquid with excitement. This was what a phantom lover was for, only this. She slipped off her chair and went to him.

Truck was sitting with his hip nudged against his chair, one foot hooked on the rung, and the other leg splayed outward in a perfect male pose—and all the more devastating because of the mat of hair that covered his belly and went lower and lower.

And as she watched, he levered himself up and undid the zipper all the way. His jeans slid down his hips and legs with the faintest erotic whisper and he kicked them away.

Carrie couldn't keep her eyes off him. She reached out to grasp him, wanting to feel him, absorb him.

He grabbed her hand before she could touch him, and he drew her in close to him. "Tell me, Carrie. Tell me what."

"You know what," she whispered.

"And nothing more," he murmured. *But dear God, he wanted it to be something more.*

He hooked the fingers of his free hand in the waistband of her shorts.

"Nothing less." He slipped them, agonizingly slowly,

from her body. She was naked underneath, naked and waiting, for him.

That was all he needed to know. He held her eyes as he braced himself and pushed against her, at the perfect angle to claim her. She moved to meet him, canting her body to receive him by lifting one of her legs over his, and easing his way in.

And then they were face-to-face, connected in the most erotic way possible, not moving, not speaking, not kissing. Just feeling the deep power of their connection, and the radiating sense of fullness. It wasn't the same frenzied coupling as the last time. It was long and almost lazy.

Carrie held on tight, letting him dictate the moves, reveling in the pleasure of his hands on her, and in the sweet slow slide of him possessing her.

Her climax came out of nowhere, one moment low and slow, the next a blowtorch of sensation that blasted her body and dissolved her right into his culmination.

Then she left him, just for a moment, just to prepare. She wanted to spend the night with him, she wanted him in her bed. But when she returned, her phantom lover had disappeared.

CARRIE ARRANGED to have lunch with Jeannie after her first day working at Longford's, and they met at the Country Roads Restaurant just outside of town.

Jeannie was dressed to sexy-lady perfection and the sight of her startled Carrie all over again.

"So," Jeannie said after they'd ordered. "What do you think?"

"I think the previous secretary made a mess of things," Carrie said. "It's going to take a while to straighten out, and to learn the ordering system. But things are slow right now, Mr. Longford tells me, so...I should have some time to learn my way around his system."

"Sounds good. Sounds like just what you needed."

"Maybe," Carrie agreed.

"Did you tell Truck you were working there?"

"No," Carrie said, more sharply than she'd intended. "Why should I?"

Jeannie grinned at her. "Why shouldn't you? Did you know he's performing at the festival Saturday with the band?"

"I didn't know that. No reason I should."

"Jeez, Carrie, the guy's working on your house for practically nothing. The least you could do is be a little neighborly."

"Well, speaking of that," Carrie said, more to distract Jeannie than to read her the riot act, "what about Tom?"

Jeannie flushed. "He's a friend. He's our vet, actually."

"And he'll be there Saturday."

"For the animals," Jeannie put in.

"Right, for the animals."

"You're tough, Carrie."

"You're more stubborn than I. You've been trying to hatch up something between me and Truck since I got home." There, throw her off the scent.

"Well, why not? I don't think he ever got over you."

"There was nothing to get over, not after fifteen years."

"I know my Trucker," Jeannie said affectionately. "Guys like him simmer forever. I told you that he usually goes out of town. Well, he hasn't been going out of town that anyone's noticed."

"For heaven's sake, Jeannie." Carrie lost her appetite.

"And if everyone knows that much about him, what do you think they know about you? Especially after all these radical changes you've made."

"They know I've made changes. They know about Eddie. They know I'm friends with Truck and Tom and about a half-dozen other guys I can think of, and they know I'm looking pretty damn good these days."

"And they're calculating that one plus four makes two," Carrie said.

"Fine if they do. It would be pretty interesting to be viewed as a *femme fatale* for a change. Ladies, hide your husbands. Jeannie Gerardo is on the town."

"Jeannie, I know you're joking, but this is serious and I feel partly responsible for it."

Jeannie dropped her sandwich. "Don't be stupid, Carrie. All you did was give me the motivation to do what I always dreamed of doing."

"Do you hear yourself? What did you always dream of doing?"

"Dressing flashier, sexier. Getting noticed. Attracting men." There was a wealth of loneliness and yearning behind her lighthearted words.

"Well, you've done that for sure," Carrie murmured, not certain where she wanted to take her objections. Maybe Jeannie wasn't talking about leaving Eddie at all. Maybe she was just trying to get his attention, and it was working, but in some perverse, unexpected way. And in the meantime, Jeannie was enjoying her new look and her newfound confidence. So why did *she* have a problem with that?

She didn't, Carrie decided. What worried her really were the long-term consequences, but no one could predict what they'd be.

"It's kinda nice, too," Jeannie said. "Getting noticed, I

mean. But that's not something you'd understand. Everyone notices you."

"Not before I got big blond hair, they didn't," Carrie said. "You have to stop thinking that I just emerged like this. *This*—me—took lots of hard work. Everything was hard for me. The business with Truck senior year. Going to college. Living away from home. Worrying about my mother. The guilt. You can't believe the guilt I felt being five hundred miles away. And the jobs. They used to start secretaries in advertising departments out on less than Longford is paying me now. And the competition was fierce. Everyone fresh out of college went right to some creative department as a secretary, hoping to get a break someday.

"Then there was the salary that never covered the rent, roommates either bad or indifferent, failed relationships, moves from agency to agency trying to better your position. And finally, the client bureaucracy that used to hang us up over every line of dialogue, every angle of a scene in the commercials. I won't even tell you how many campaigns got trashed. How many focus groups dictated what the client would advertise."

"Then why," Jeannie said, puzzled by her passion, "were you ever in that business?"

"Because..." Did she really know why? Carrie wondered. Had she ever known? Was it purely the risk of walking on the edge of the knife every day? Had she been doing *anything* creative in the last few years, really, that she could justify her need to sacrifice herself all over again?

And she would do so again, in a heartbeat when the call came.

"Because," she said again, "that's what I wanted to do, I guess. I mean, it sounded just as glamorous from my standpoint as it sounds from yours. And it's not. It probably never was."

"So don't go back. If they ask you."

That thought was inconceivable. *If* they asked her? *When.*

"Maybe," Carrie said as they got ready to leave. *Never.*

THE BEAN-HOLE BEAN FESTIVAL was an annual event, always held on the last weekend in July. It was a combination of crafts fair, carnival and competition. There was music all weekend long in the picnic grounds where the beans, which had been baking underground for a week under the eye of the bean master, were served with hot dogs, hamburgers, ribs and steaks.

In the barn, local crafts and cakes and pies, were up for judging on the first and last days of the festival, and nearby, local artists and artisans set up booths selling their wares. Friday afternoon, the carnival and sideshow opened; Saturday, there were the horse trials, pig scrambles, truck and tractor pulls, cow-chip bingo, and beans, beans and more beans.

Friday night was family night as well. Everyone went to the carnival. Everyone took a chance on a prize.

Saturday things got more serious.

"Even Eddie participates in the truck pull. Most of the guys do," Jeannie told her as they drove toward the fairgrounds which were spread out over a dozen acres behind the old Paradise shopping center. "Well, here you go. This is why you have to come early. Everybody's here."

It was nine o'clock in the morning and crowded as a city street. Music was going, and the amusement-park rides were packed. Everywhere you looked there were families, children carrying stuffed animals and cotton candy, and their parents trying to keep up and keep an eye on them.

"Truck's going on at ten," Jeannie said. "He's doing the truck pull, second heat."

Why don't I know that? Carrie thought. *Why couldn't I have known that?*

They strolled down the midway, stopping here and there to watch someone try to win a prize. It was a portable amusement park with rides and stalls that had been set up practically overnight. But it was no less exciting and alluring to this crowd who had come to have fun.

Jeannie bought her some cotton candy. "Have you ever had this since you were six?"

"I don't think so." Carrie closed her mouth over a sugar puff of it. "Oh my God. I'm going to have a sugar fit."

"Just shut up and don't analyze it."

"Yes, ma'am."

They went on, and Carrie noticed people looking at Jeannie. And why not? The bodysuit fit her like a glove and, paired with the long, seemingly demure skirt and the big bold jewelry, gave her both an appealing and a seductive air.

Men were *noticing*.

They followed the crowd toward the bandstand.

"I don't suppose you're up for beans this early in the morning," Jeannie asked.

"Oh, I could stand to eat a bowl, I suppose."

"And we can get some to take home, too."

They queued up opposite the kettle, which was still buried in the ground, and the line inched forward as the bean master doled out endless bowls and containers.

They got two quarts to take home besides, and settled at a picnic table close to the stage to eat.

"Oh, look, there's Truck."

Words to make Carrie feel like an anxious seventeen-year-old.

Truck vaulted off the stage to join them, and Carrie had a flashing vision of him with his jeans sinking downward over his...before his voice broke in and startled her.

"How're you doing, Carrie?"

"I'm okay," she murmured.

"Did you know Carrie started working over at Longford's?" Jeannie put in.

"Actually I did," Truck said, holding Carrie's gaze. "Old Man told me."

Why couldn't I tell you?

"Have you tried these beans? They're great this year. Taste them. I bet you didn't eat anything this morning." Jeannie held her spoon to his lips and he flicked out his tongue.

Carrie felt an unexpected spiral of arousal. *Why should Jeannie get to do that for you?*

"I think you're right," Truck said. "They're really good this year."

Jeannie licked her spoon and slanted a glance at Carrie. "Do you like 'em?"

"Delicious," she murmured. *What were they really talking about?*

But Truck wasn't talking to her at all.

"When are you on?" Jeannie asked him.

"In about ten minutes," he said, looking at his watch, then looking over at Carrie. "I'd better go."

I come in the depths of the night so you don't have to seen with me, you don't have to talk to me...

He meant it, she thought. He really meant it.

She clenched her hands. She had never felt such a volatile jealousy before. And all over Jeannie and her cleavage and her friend's long friendship with Truck.

Carrie settled back at the table, trying to keep her emotions in check. She wondered, what if she whistled...?

They sat through two sets, watching him play, and Carrie felt every movement of his hands right down in her vitals. There was something inordinately sexy about the way he bent over his fiddle with such intensity. Something so vitally erotic and electric in the way he played.

And the crowd's response. Women and girls particularly.

Or maybe she was overstating the case.

He hasn't gone out of town recently...

Afterward, they walked to the back field together, and Truck got ready for the competition while Carrie and Jeannie found a seat in the crowded noisy grandstand.

Dust flew everywhere as the trucks roared up to the starting line.

"They're truckin' about a thousand pounds back there," Jeannie said. "They go two by two, whoever moves it over there wins." She pointed to a pole fifty yards away.

"And guys ruin their engines competing in this?"

Jeannie looked taken aback. "I guess they do. Oh look, there's Eddie. He's going off in the second round. And Truck is right behind him."

It was, Carrie supposed, a fascinating male contest: to be the one to drive the machine that moved the most weight in the least amount of time with the least damage to the drive shaft and engine.

The crowd was really getting into it. Clearly, they had their favorites, and there was wild applause as Eddie Gerardo and his opponent drove up to the starting line and the pallets of bar weights were attached to the underside of their trucks.

"Ed-die, Ed-die—" The chant started, steady and rhythmic. The starter popped his gun. Eddie and his opponent gunned their engines, and slowly, slowly, they each moved off the starting line, churning up dirt and dust everywhere. It must have taken a full ten minutes for either truck to move forward, and then it was all about the driver's skill in handling his vehicle, and getting the advantage. Another ten minutes, and it was over, and Eddie had lost the round.

"Poor Eddie," Jeannie murmured. "He was in the finals last year. So was Truck—there he is."

It was a different story, Carrie found, when you were rooting for someone. Of course, there were three dozen others who wanted him to win just as ferociously as she, and they chanted loudly behind her: "Truck, Truck, Truck..." as he rolled up to the starting line, the pallet was attached, and the gun went off.

Truck was determined. Jeannie told her he'd won with it last year, and sure enough, as he and his opponent plowed through the dust and grass, he inched ahead and over the finish line.

"Finals tomorrow," Jeannie said to Carrie over the applause. "Seen enough?"

Truck joined them a few minutes later, beating the dust from his shirt and hair. "I have to check on Old Man. Want to come?"

Old Man was in the adjunct barn playing bingo. It was one of his enduring pleasures, whether he went into town to the Masonic Hall, or just milled around with a group of fair-goers he didn't know. By the time the session was over, he got to know them pretty well.

He was deep in a game when Truck touched his elbow.

"Hey, son."

"Think you can afford to drop a game? Carrie and Jeannie are here."

"Oh sure." Old Man wheeled around to see them standing in the doorway. A moment later, he was grasping Carrie's hands, stunning her with his strength and vitality, and his resemblance to Truck.

"Carrie. Welcome home, my dear."

It was the eyes, she thought. No, the mouth. The voice. Definitely the voice. There was nothing infirm about Old Man, nor did his wheelchair seem to limit him. If anything, you hardly noticed it once you were captivated by his voice.

"I was so sorry about your mother. So sorry. She was so brave, Carrie. I hope that's some comfort to you. It's good to see you, good to have you here. Tell me, did Truck invite you up for dinner?"

She felt a wash of shame. "I think he tried."

Old Man gave her a sharp look. "But now you'll come, won't you?"

"I will," she whispered. How could she deny him when it had nothing to do with Truck at all.

Old Man smiled, and it was Truck's smile, Truck's face, thirty years older. How could anyone not love him? she thought.

How could anyone not love Truck—

Oh no, she didn't want to go there, she couldn't.

"Good," Old Man was saying. "And soon, Carrie."

"I will," she promised. *What* was she promising?

"You know we've been talking on a regular basis recently?"

"How so?"

"Longford's my local supplier."

"Ah—" that explained that. But it didn't explain Old Man, and how warm and secure he made her feel. How she was falling for him already and she'd barely spoken to him for five minutes.

But everyone loved Old Man, and as he took Jeannie's hand, Carrie saw why.

Old Man saw everything.

"How you doing, Jeannie?" he murmured. "You look beautiful today. Don't know about you, but I like the change. And it's about time, too."

"I know," Jeannie said, tears edging around her eyes.

Old Man saw them. "You did the right thing, Jeannie. You know it. Everyone knows it. Now it's about time for me to get back to my game," he added, to spare Jeannie, who was surreptitiously wiping away her tears.

"Excuse me, won't you? Carrie, we'll see you soon?"

"Isn't he something," Jeannie said as Truck wheeled him away. "And you know what he did after the accident, after the diagnosis? He just went on ahead. Truck moved the business to the house, and Old Man took over the office. He does all the paperwork, the cost specs, the pricing, the ordering. He learned to use a computer and everything."

"Truck is very devoted."

"Yeah, well, Old Man was mom and dad to Truck. I don't know if you ever heard the story, but his mom went away. Fell for the man, but not for the life. Didn't want to live in some backwater town. But I tell you, Old Man must have been something back then, if he attracted a woman like that."

Jeannie slanted a considering look at her. "Kind of like you, actually."

Carrie froze. *No, nothing like her; she'd been raised in Paradise. It wasn't the same thing at all.* "What happened to her?" She could barely get the words out.

"She died, oh, a year or two later, I think. A car accident in Europe. Which was the kind of high life she led. I always thought she married Old Man to escape something but I guess it caught up with her in the end."

Why didn't she know this? Carrie wondered. It was one of those tragic stories that people fed on for years that became part of the town folklore. And she hadn't ever known.

"So Truck had to have been a baby when she died," she murmured, thinking how similar his loss was to her own circumstances. But that was way before she and her mother had come to Paradise.

"Five, I think."

"How do you *know* all this?" Carrie asked.

"Oh, people talk," Jeannie said airily.

Everyone knows...

I wonder what they're saying about me...

9

CARRIE AND JEANNIE ended up spending the entire weekend at the festival, not that it was planned. But they both wanted to see Truck run the finals and the judging of the crafts fair. Besides, there was some jewelry Jeannie wanted to look at, and some other odds and ends she wanted to buy. All those were in addition to attending the winddown of the live performances, which always featured a fairly well-known country star.

To get good seats close to the stage, they arrived long before the performance was scheduled to begin. By this time, Jeannie was loaded with packages, more containers of beans and no energy at all to do anything more than put up her feet and relax. Carrie was feeling pretty mellow herself. The final round of the truck pull held at noon had been exciting, exhausting and extremely hot. At least today, she'd been smart and brought a hat, a thermos of ice and bandannas for both her and Jeannie to tie around their necks. And now she was dribbling the last of the ice water onto her bandanna so she could mop her face with it while Jeannie roused herself to buy some sodas.

A body dropped down beside her. "Well, aren't you the cutest thing?" Eddie Gerardo said.

Carrie suppressed a shudder. "Hi, Eddie. Sorry you lost."

"Sure you are. Sure. But that damn race isn't the only

thing I lost. Since you got back here, I lost my wife. I want to know what kind of voodoo you're working on her, and I want you to stop it."

There was no arguing with Eddie, Carrie thought, and she wasn't even going to try. He was as predictable as the sun, and just as hot right now.

"You tell Jeannie to get rid of all that trashy stuff she's been flaunting around town, you hear me? That's not my wife in those tight clothes. That's some big-city tar—"

"Eddie." Jeannie arrived, like the cavalry, just in the nick of time. "I thought you had an appointment with the Howell sisters."

"Well, I did, that's for damn sure. But how am I going to sell them on a house in a country town if my *wife* won't advertise those plain country values?"

"Gee, I don't know," Jeannie said. "I thought you were a better salesman than that."

Eddie gave her a dirty look and stalked off.

"He sure doesn't like my new look," Jeannie said, an understatement if ever Carrie heard one.

"How far are you going to push it?" she asked curiously.

"I'm in for the duration. I wouldn't go back to being frumpy if you paid me."

The concert started soon after that; it was packed, even with extra seating, but everyone could hear the music from anywhere on the fairgrounds. The singer was a homegrown talent who had been considered a one-hit wonder, and was now making a comeback by playing local and state fairs to rebuild his audience.

He was charmisatic, and generous too, calling on local musicians to come on stage and jam, so that his set turned into an evening of extraordinary music. Truck and his band were up there with them, and that, as much as anything, kept Carrie glued to her seat. He played with unbelievable passion and power, and the give-and-take between him and the singer had the audience on its feet.

Afterward, there were autographs and interviews, and side groups making music, the milling crowd surging back to the midway for one last ride, and teenagers making plans for later on that night.

"We used to do that," Jeannie said with a laugh.

Carrie smiled. "You remember that far back?"

"Nothing changes," Jeannie said, and Carrie remembered having believed that the day she rode into town. But things did change: people, circumstances, the landscape of your dreams.

And the things you thought you wanted fell like dominoes before the things you could realistically have.

Carrie didn't look back once as she and Jeannie exited the fairgrounds.

TRUCK HAD the warrior princess imprisoned in the tower and so confused she didn't quite know what to do.

But she was coming around, Truck thought as he got up the next morning. The job at Longford's was the first step, and she'd taken it all on her own. She wasn't going anywhere any too soon except into his bed. And into his life.

Every time he saw her, it was like adding fuel to the fire. Yesterday, tonight, he wanted to be with her, and instead he had been held up by a group of admiring musicians and he'd played the damn night long with a bunch of guys he'd never see again in this lifetime.

The choices a man had to make...

But Carrie was going to have to make choices too

whether she wanted to or not. This thing between them was escalating by the minute, and it wasn't just about desire. There was something more, something deeper, and he was damned if he was the only one feeling it.

Carrie had to be feeling it too, or she wouldn't be responding to him the way she was. That was the thing he was counting on. That deeper connection, the one she wouldn't acknowledge, the one she refused to let into the light of the day. Well, it didn't matter what she called it. Or what she thought was happening between them, deep in the night. He knew the truth, he knew what it was, and he knew eventually she would fall.

Over breakfast, Old Man told him, "Longford says she's given the place some class. Makes him look good. And she's gettin' through the mess, he says. Gettin' everything on spreadsheets and databases. He can finally see the desk, he says."

"All that in a week?" Truck said admiringly. "She's a wonder." But maybe it was more than that. Maybe Carrie was just someone who got things done. She'd worked under pressure and deadlines, and it could be said that her job had been to solve problems. Overhauling someone's office system probably wasn't much different, and a damn sight easier, than dealing with jittery clients.

Now all she had to learn to do was overhaul her life.

"Get her up to dinner," Old Man said. "Listen to me, son. Don't lose her."

"Soon," Truck promised. "Soon."

WORK, Carrie thought. You couldn't depend on a *phantom lover*, but you could always depend on work.

She'd been a Longford's about a week and already she had found some real satisfaction in setting up some basic office systems and procedures. It was instant gratification. Mr. Longford said either no or yes and the thing was done. She had forgotten the world could work that way.

By the sixth day, she had cleared all the extraneous papers from the desk and either filed them or entered the information on a spreadsheet, and she was working on a payroll spreadsheet for Mrs. Longford. And she was also helping out in the store, and she found a certain enjoyment in that too.

She learned that the Heaths were putting a two-story addition on their house with a bath, they said, and Truck was going to do the plumbing; and that Mr. Emberly had a chronic sink problem, but Mr. Longford said he only came in because he wanted company. She met Maria Bonnell, the carpenter, and Junie de Longo, the artist who designed custom-made frames.

She heard Mrs. Williams was ailing—Al the tile man couldn't get into her house to finish up her porch floor; and that the Hillmans were retiring and selling their summer home for the kind of money that hadn't been dreamed of in this town before and Eddie Gerardo was handling the sale.

At one time or another, a whole range of townspeople came in that door looking for a pair of pliers, a screwdriver, a glue gun, advice on how to hang wallpaper, or fix a door that squeaked.

And to chat. Carrie was amazed that customers had time to stand around and chat, to ask after someone's family, to give some details about their own. To talk about what was going on in town, in local politics, in Washington, and the world. And sometimes, someone would talk to her about her mother. Then after the social chat was all over, there was still time to get back to work.

She'd never done business that way, and was surprised by how much she liked it.

People knew her now. They waved when she came out of the store at noon, and as she roared up Main Street on her way home. They greeted her in the supermarket and at the post office where those sorry-we-found-another-candidate-more-qualified-than-you letters kept dribbling in.

There wasn't going to be a call from New York, she thought, or Boston or L.A., and she began distancing herself from the disappointment those letters brought her.

What she had here and now was enough, she thought; she could build from there.

TRUCK CAME to Longford's a day later to pick up some adhesive Old Man had special-ordered. It was about fifteen minutes before noon. The store was quiet, Henry Longford was going over some papers, and he motioned Truck to the back of the store.

Truck hadn't seen Carrie since the weekend, hadn't had time for anything but work and the gnawing yearning that was his constant companion whenever he thought about her. He was damn intrigued by the daily reports Old Man was giving him about how she had taken over Longford's back room, and he was curious to see Carrie in her new realm.

She was checking a printout against some handwritten numbers as he came to the door. And she looked fabulous, dressed in a classy cobalt-blue silk dress, accented with chunky silver jewelry.

Carrie could feel him there, looming, sending her senses into a tailspin. Why today, why now? She looked up, girding herself to be calm and collected, the sexy-lady way. "Hi, Truck."

She was good, he had to give her that. He didn't know any other woman who could maintain that disdainful tone in the face of all the heat they had generated. But a warrior princess had to have a cool head especially when she was trapped. Especially when they generated sparks just by looking at each other.

So Truck didn't waste words. He had more potent weapons. "That adhesive Old Man ordered?"

"It's in," she said coolly, wholly aware of the heat and tension between them. Instant on, like the flick of a remote. "In the back. Jerry will know."

What was it about him? she thought, unable to keep her eyes off him. It was easier to think that Truck was the sum of his parts—the tight jeans, the cotton shirt slung casually over the black T-shirt, those knowing eyes, those wicked workman's hands...

Don't go there—

"Put it on my account."

An insanely unsatisfactory conversation.

"Done," she murmured. *If that's how he wants things to be...*

"Thanks." The ball was in her court, Truck thought, his body tight with desire. She could not mistake that he wanted her, that right now, this instant he wanted her. But she was so damn determined to have it all her way, to hide, suppress and deny everything that was between them. What else could a warrior princess do when she was backed against the wall?

Carrie had turned her attention back to the pages she'd been scanning and he gazed at her for one long moment more before he turned and walked out the door.

He was almost at the store warehouse when he heard the long low sound of her faltering whistle.

NOW WHAT?

Carrie was shaking at her audacity. After this many days, after there had been no contact, after he'd said he was willing and then he practically ignored her, what did a woman do?

She whistled.

...so you never have to be seen with me, you never have to talk to me...

Taking her at her word. Giving her exactly what she'd said she wanted.

And it was so damn unsatisfactory she wanted to scream.

What *did* she want?

The phone rang. She jumped.

Jeannie. Lunch.

"Not today," Carrie said, swallowing hard. "I have some stuff to get done today."

Stuff. Truck was now relegated to the bin labeled *stuff.*

...I'm willing—tonight and any night...a hot body in the dark and no contact during the day...I'm willing—

If he had heard her. If he even still wanted her.

I'm willing, she thought, a stifling excitement catching her breath. *Anywhere. Anytime.* Her body went liquid just thinking about it, just imagining it.

It didn't matter where. It didn't matter when.

What did you call that?

What name did you put to this hot need that could only be filled by him?

Carrie wanted him and she'd asked. When he came, she'd be waiting.

TRUCK CAUGHT UP with her before she left town on her cycle, running her down near the supermarket parking lot.

"Park that thing and get in here."

Her throat went dry; she grabbed the first space she saw, and a minute later, she climbed in beside him.

He was in a fury, edgy, sexy, slightly out of control.

"Don't say a word. I have no time today, none. I've got twenty minutes. Yes or no?"

She felt a thrill go down her spine. "Yes," she whispered.

He gunned his way down Route 30 toward the Pond Road at an obscene speed. "There's no time, no goddamn time..." He swerved down the track to her house, jammed on the brake and cut the engine.

"Get over here." He pulled her to him. His kiss was raw with need. He pushed the seat backward, as far as it would go, and he plundered her mouth, his left hand cupping her breast, feeling for the taut point of her nipple.

Immediately, her body eased as the familiar molten sensation streamed from that pleasure point and pooled between her legs.

She needed this, she wanted this. She couldn't live without this, without him.

Without him?

Had it come to that—already?

"Let's go in the house."

Carrie could barely move, her knees were so weak, her body so aroused. She barely made it into the bedroom before he had off his jeans. Her excitement escalated. He was so big, so thick, so *there*. Her hands shook as she took off her dress and underthings.

"I've been like this all morning. I can't wait." He reached over for her.

She sank onto the bed, and he came after her.

Pushing, pushing, pushing, rocking against her, murmuring against her ear, her mouth, *yes, yes, yes*...taking her mouth again as she yielded everything to him and his ferocious need.

"You're so hot, you're always so hot."

"For you," she whispered.

He caught his breath at the words. *She knew it, she knew it, thank God, she knew it.*

"Good," he whispered back, slowing down his rush to completion. "Why do you think?"

"I don't want to think," she murmured. "I can't think...."

Words to drive him crazy, drive her crazy. It would be so easy to let go, right now, to give in to his overwhelming need to drown himself in her, just as he had intended when he'd intercepted her. Suddenly he didn't want to; suddenly he wanted to forget everything he had to do today, and just stay with her all day and all night long.

Too much, too soon. It wasn't enough. It was starting not to be nearly enough.

So what did you call that? What would she?

Or did they have to define this powerful connection at all?

Truck shifted his weight. This was all the definition he needed: his body imprinted on hers, as close as a man could get, no mistaking what he wanted and what he felt, and with that thought he came, his body jolting against hers, and wished it was forever.

OLD MRS. SWANSON DIED, and Carrie went to the funeral. Jerry, the gangly teenager who worked the front of the store, was headed off to college, so Carrie took over some of his duties.

Mrs. Longford got sick. Carrie did the payroll. She learned the stock. She modified the ad that Longford's ran in the local paper. She rearranged the front of the store.

She lunched with Jeannie frequently, and sometimes with Jeannie's friends. They went to the movies, out to dinner, or shopping at the outlet malls. She went to the theater, to concerts, and museums.

She painted her living room and bedroom, rearranged the furniture, bought a new coffeemaker and priced a used car.

But when she found herself considering an evening course at the high school in the fall, she knew something had changed.

She didn't know what, and she didn't know why, but suddenly it seemed as if she really was planning to stay.

The second week after her Longford's ad ran in the paper, Tom came to the store to ask if she would design an ad for him.

She was already working on the chamber of commerce project, and she suddenly felt as if she was flexing her creative muscles for the first time in a long time.

"But you're not going to leave us." Mr. Longford had said when she'd told him about doing the ad for Tom as an outgrowth of what she'd done for the store.

"No. I'm enjoying it too much." She had heard herself say the words, she had been shocked she said the words, realizing that she really meant them.

"Well, the place grows on you," Jeannie had said when Carrie related the conversation to her over the phone that evening. "Maybe you have to grow up to appreciate it."

"Maybe you have to grow up altogether," Carrie had

said wryly. "Maybe the years in New York were my teenage years."

"So what about your teenage crush?" Jeannie had murmured. "Don't deny it. I've seen the way he looks at you."

Carrie had groaned. "Maybe I'll know it's serious when he brings me home to Old Man."

All she could think about was Truck as she sat at the kitchen table, trying to come up with a snappy ad for Tom's vet service. But Truck hadn't made a move to ask her, even after Old Man's prodding. He was a thief in the night, stealing her heart, her soul, drugging her up with his prowess and his passion.

This is what you want...just whistle—

Was it what she wanted? It was so much easier this way. He gave her everything she could handle and more. But she couldn't have his nights, and she couldn't have his days. And when they met on the street, he was courteous and noncommittal.

So you never have to be seen with me, you never have to talk to me, you never have to make a commitment to me—

She was greedy for him, and wary of his power.

And she chafed against her self-imposed restrictions, knowing in her heart she wanted more, more and more.

But if she gave in to her deepest emotions, she knew exactly what the end would be, and as much as she hated it, she knew she wanted her freedom more.

THE CHAMBER OF COMMERCE voted to accept her proposal for a promotion piece extolling the trilake area of Segers, Paradise and Hunter Cove that would be distributed to travel agents and run as an insert in papers all over the country the following June.

Now she was really busy and brimming with ideas.

"Carrie doesn't have time now for her *old* friends," Jeannie teased her one night when they were out to dinner with some of Jeannie's friends.

"And where is Eddie tonight?" one of the women asked.

"Making a *sale*," another one commented, and everyone laughed.

Jeannie laughed. "Hey, some of those working couples can't come to see a house except at night."

"Yeah, but Eddie," a woman named Mavis said. She turned to Carrie. "We've telling her for years to dump the guy. And now that she's looking sharp and sexy, what does she decide to do? Give him *another* chance."

"Jeannie knows what she's doing," Carrie said staunchly. But did she? This whole sexy-lady business had turned everything inside out for Jeannie who was still covering up her heartbreak. If Eddie was doing anything untoward, no one knew about it, but obviously these friends did.

"He's selling a house," Jeannie said.

"Okay, okay." Mavis threw up her hands. "He's selling a house."

"Or he may not be," Jeannie said later as she drove Carrie home. "Maybe he's not. Chances are he isn't. So what does that make me, after all these years?"

"Loving. Trusting. Faithful. Loyal." *Trapped.* And Carrie felt disloyal thinking that. *But hadn't she been feeling that way too?* "What are you going to do?"

She didn't know what to do.

"I don't know," Jeannie said. "I think he blames you for what he calls my liberated tendencies. He thinks I've had a brainstorm or something."

"He was never the brightest guy," Carrie said tentatively. "What does he expect?"

"That marriages last forever."

"That's pie in the sky."

"Mom's apple pie. His parents have been together fifty years, if you can imagine it. He can't picture anything less, as long as anything goes for him."

"I'm sorry, Jeannie."

"It's okay. It was going on long before you came back. Everybody knows." She pulled into the track down to the house. "Here we are. See you tomorrow."

"Take care." Oh, but how did you take care of a situation like Eddie? How did Jeannie stand it? How did any woman?

Never, Carrie vowed. It was just that kind of thing that made her so wary. *Never. No man would ever trap her like that.*

And then she walked into her house to find Truck, naked, waiting in her bedroom.

I HAVE TO COOL THIS DOWN. This is going nowhere. I don't want it to go anywhere. I have to cool this down.

Carrie sat at her desk in Longford's, drawing circles all over the blank page of a pad. Jeannie's situation was driving her crazy. And her own was driving her mad.

She was not in love with Truck. She wasn't, she wasn't, she wasn't.

Actually, I thought it was love...

Those words had torn her up. What did he think it was now? Lust. No, that wasn't right. She was the one who didn't want to get involved.

And she didn't want to remember the pleasure of looking at him, being with him last night.

Why couldn't things be simple, without emotions getting in the way?

She had to end this...this "thing" with Truck. It was doing neither of them any good. And it wasn't as if Truck hadn't known from the outset how she felt about things.

The problem was more didn't equal less. Having more just made her want more. But more of what? She didn't want to answer that question, because she would have to give away too much.

Therefore, she would give up Truck.

All right. That was point number one on her list of things to do.

Number two—work. Tom's ad; the mock-up of the presentation piece for the chamber of commerce. She was a day or two behind on that.

Number three—Jeannie. She should check on Jeannie and make sure she was okay.

Number four—end this *thing* with Truck.

Number five—end it, and then make sure *she* would be okay.

"EDDIE WAS," Jeannie said. "He was with a client."

"And you know this—how?" Carrie said, impatiently twirling the phone cord as she sat at her desk at Longford's.

"I saw them. I went by the office—I don't normally do that anymore, but I did. After I left you, I went by the office, and he was there, with them. So he didn't lie."

"You're sure?"

Jeannie sighed. "Look, you know the worst of it now, so why would I cover for him?"

"Because you're so used to doing it," Carrie said.

"Not anymore," Jeannie said. "Never anymore."

So that was that. For today. But why oh why couldn't Eddie be the husband that Jeannie wanted? Carrie wondered, finding it hard to concentrate after talking to Jeannie. Why wasn't anything in life clear-cut?

She would never understand men like that; but it was also true that she knew nothing of the dynamics of their marriage. Nothing about how they related to each other.

Nothing about anything, even my life.

Even so, her life seemed to be going more smoothly than she anticipated. In mid-August, she finished the final version of the trilake proposal, and two more local businesses recruited her to expand their statewide advertising on the basis of the ads she'd done for Longford's.

She was beginning to think she might make a little career here.

And she'd still done nothing about Truck.

No, not so. She had allowed herself to drift along. That was what she'd done about Truck. She'd just plain left things the way they were.

Time for a change.

But where and when, she didn't know because whatever work Truck was doing on her house now, he was doing while she was at Longford's. It was almost as if he was shielding her from any gossip about all the things they did in the dark.

He was protecting her.

Carrie ran into him one afternoon at the Country Roads Restaurant. The very crowded Country Roads Restaurant. Where there weren't any seats around about noon, and where everybody knew each other.

Truck was in a booth alone. And he saw the light of battle in Carrie's eyes. "Have a seat, Carrie."

"I don't think so." She looked around her. She couldn't even say she wanted to talk to him some other time or place without someone overhearing it. "Thanks anyway. I just want some...some coffee, and then I'm going home."

"Sit *down*."

There was a tone that brooked no resistance. She sank into the booth.

"You're crazy, you know."

"Have a fry." He held out one to her and she pushed his hand away.

She never pushed his hands away, ever. She begged for his hands over and over...

Stop *it!* "Stop it."

"Sure." He swiped the French fry with ketchup and popped it into his mouth. "What's on your mind?"

"Nothing we can discuss here," she whispered fiercely, arrested by the movement of his mouth. *The mouth she knew better than her own. The mouth that gave the most luscious kisses. Oh, dear Lord...*"Nothing. Just nothing."

This was what it would be like to be in public with him. This, with all the sumptuous memories between them. She would have to move to another town, Carrie thought. She wouldn't be able to stand it. She would always be poised on the edge of either jumping into his arms or just walking away.

And either decision scared her half to death.

"I lost my appetite," she said faintly.

"I haven't lost mine." He tossed some money on the table. "Come on," he said with exaggerated care, just in case anyone was listening, "I'll show you where we're at on your house and how much we've gotten done."

"So here's the deal," Carrie said as she faced him across the kitchen counter. "We have to stop."

Truck looked at her for a long, long time, trying to gauge how serious she was. She was serious. The warrior princess had found a weapon that cut the enemy right off at the knees: the word *no*.

He didn't take that lightly either. He knew how conflicted she was, how torn. How scared. And he knew how hard it was for her to do what she was doing, even without the burden of the secret assignations with him. It was only a matter of time, he thought. Neither of them could stop, really. But if she wanted to try, he was perfectly willing to let her.

For a day.

And that was a tactic he was sure *she* didn't expect.

"Okay," he said.

She started. "*Okay? That's it? Okay?*"

"That's it. We've always operated on what *you* want, Carrie. So, if this is it—this is it." *She didn't like that. Good—it was a start.*

She felt as if someone had just punched her. "Oh."

"We won't do the friend thing either. I wouldn't embarrass you like that." *Even better—she hated that.*

Better with me—or without me, Carrie? Think about it. Imagine it.

She was imagining it too well.

"No," she said faintly.

Carrie had expected some protest, some argument, some sensual persuasion. But this calm acceptance of her decision knocked her for a loop. She didn't know what else to say. She almost felt as if she couldn't leave it hanging in the air like that.

We have to stop.

Okay.

There was something too cavalier about that, almost as if he could automatically disengage his emotions. Or maybe they'd never been engaged?

No! She knew him. She *knew* him. And he'd always been there, in command, and fully engaged.

Her confusion was endearing. Truck wanted to wrap her in his arms and tell her she didn't have to make that decision, that she didn't have to be so scared. But he wasn't going to. This was the pressure point, he thought. This was the moment when she would realize that what was between them wasn't just secret sex.

And maybe it took something as catastrophic as this. He hoped to hell it did, because he planned to be back in bed with her tomorrow night, and she'd better have decided that was exactly where she wanted him.

God, it was such a dicey long shot.

"Anything else, Carrie?" he asked into her stunned silence.

"No." She hated men, just *hated* them. Truck was going to walk off without even trying to salvage something, as if all those nights meant nothing to him. That was what men did.

That was why she had to be free.

"Okay." He could see she was floundering, she was furious and one tiny particle of her was relieved. But he wasn't going to make it easy. "Well, I'll finish up in the house as soon I can, and I guess I'll see you at the store."

"Right." She held on tight, tight, tight to her emotions as he stepped out the door.

Truck knew he couldn't leave her like that. He didn't want to leave her at all. If she just made one move, one subtle concession, he would stay with her forever.

"Carrie?"

"*What?*"

He threw her a verbal bone. "We had some spectacular nights."

"Did we? I hadn't noticed," she said as calmly as she could as Truck walked out the door…and out of her life.

She wasn't crying, she wasn't, but as he revved the engine of the van, she felt the tears streaming down her face.

It was better this way. All these feelings she'd been having, all this yearning for *more*. She knew what that was, really. It was the *moreness* of being a couple, of admitting there was something beyond their luscious coupling that linked them.

She had been sinking in quicksand all these weeks.

But now she was on firm ground. She had come to her senses.

No more men. No more wild forbidden sex.

Actually, I thought it was love…

10

CARRIE'S DAYS HAD TAKEN on a certain structure. She went to Longford's every morning and stayed until two. She'd taken on the increased hours at Mr. Longford's request so she could relieve him and Mrs. Longford for lunch, and because she liked that time in the front of the store. It wasn't busy, but there were enough customers to keep it interesting. And she was learning all about hardware-store stock.

Of course, there were the customers who greeted her like an old friend. "Hey, Carrie, how you doing? You got some window putty?" "I need a pound of tenpenny nails." "I need some solder. I swear I've looked everywhere..." "Foam brushes?" "Enamel paint, small can?" "One-fifty-grade sandpaper?"

All these things she had learned and more.

"Hi, George, how's your wife?"

"Thanks for asking, Carrie. She's doing well. Home from the hospital tomorrow. Gonna have a little celebration. You're welcome to come."

"'Morning, Junie," to the woman who owned the framing shop. "You after some gold-leaf paint today?"

"And some angle braces, screws, brown paper, oh, I need glue sticks...let me see, well, you take the list," June said.

"'Afternoon, Callie," to the woman who worked in the thrift shop across the street. "I heard you've got some paintings in the Hunter Cove art show end of August."

"You bet," Callie said. "I just had a booth down in Rockport. I sold two paintings, so I'm hoping for good things at this show too."

It was also nice, Carrie discovered, getting a regular paycheck again. The only drawback to her work schedule was she saw Jeannie only when she went to make deposits at the bank.

Today Jeannie was looking a little drawn, as if some of her sexy-lady persona had been sapped out of her.

"Are you okay?"

"I'm okay. Eddie's been pressuring me a little. He says my new image isn't good for business. That prospective customers look at me and wonder what's going on in Paradise." Jeannie counted out the money she was returning with an emphatic snap. "We've been *discussing* it."

"Sounds like you haven't been *talking*."

"No," Jeannie said tiredly. "We've been shouting."

"I'm going to take you out to dinner Friday night," Carrie said decisively. "You need to get out."

"It's a date." Jeannie handed her the money. "I don't want to go back to where I was. I like where I am now."

"I know. I know." Carrie hated leaving her but she had a schedule to maintain. Between two and three, she did her banking, her shopping and any other little chores that required her to be in town.

Ideally, she tried to be home by four. She then changed into casual clothes and set up either at her desk or on the porch where she had rigged up a work surface on two sawhorses where she could look out over the pond. There on those mid-August hot, hazy afternoons, she laid out all the projects she'd taken on and worked outside until sundown.

She loved the luxury of having time. Time seemed to stretch, suddenly, to encompass her day, and if she wanted to just sit sometimes and contemplate the pond, she had time to do that too. And time to think about what she was doing and how, rather than being at the mercy of deadlines, nerves, office politics and clocks. It was a new experience for her to have this kind of time; and she felt it gave her a kind of freedom because she was suddenly doing the work she loved to do, but without all the complications she'd been so used to.

At six o'clock, she made dinner, usually a salad or sautéed chicken or some pasta, and ate while listening to the news or reading the paper.

After dinner, she went on-line or she worked. Ten o'clock to midnight, Carrie read—women's magazines, industry magazines, mysteries, commercial fiction, anything to take her mind off Truck. Anything to keep her going through the long nights.

It would get easier. A *phantom lover* couldn't be depended upon anyway. It had been a liaison doomed to burn itself out.

Except she felt herself still flaring up at odd times during the night, and sometimes during the day. Yet the thought of Jeannie's situation and the price that Jeannie was going to have to pay, invariably doused her ardor.

Jeannie was in a wry humor when they settled in at a brand-new upscale restaurant the following Friday. "Let me tell you, Old Man gave me an earful when I was over to Truck's for dinner the other night."

"No kidding. Old Man?"

"He's got a pipeline from that back office in his house to all over the county, and he knows everything," Jeannie said as she played with her fork. "He says it's time to go."

Was it? Carrie wondered. Was this the foreordained conclusion to what she and Jeannie lightheartedly had started two months ago?

Two months? Had it really been two months? She had no answers for Jeannie. Her life was just as messed up.

"That sounds pretty radical coming from someone like Old Man."

"He says I could run the business, and better than Eddie too."

"I bet you could," Carrie said feelingly.

"They give real-estate courses at the night school. I think I'm gonna enroll."

"Okay. I thought I might take some courses myself."

"Good. We'll do it together," Jeannie said.

So there it was, Jeannie's life was rolling forward in a way she couldn't possibly have anticipated, and all because she got trapped with the wrong man.

Consequences. Everything had consequences, for Jeannie especially. Eddie might see this as a further betrayal but if Jeannie was seriously thinking of leaving him, she might want to make even more drastic changes in her life.

"I went through Eddie's books," Jeannie said suddenly. "The firm should be doing better, you know. And he's just been maintaining a certain level. Well, that's because he's been redirecting some of the money to cover expenses, and I bet you can guess what they are."

"Wine, women and song," Carrie said immediately, feeling a clutch of anger.

"Yeah. That's how it looks. So, it's time to stop being a doormat. But I don't know if I'm strong enough to do that."

"You're strong," Carrie said encouragingly. "You've got a hundred friends who'll support you."

"Except I don't know how it's going to play out once I confront him."

"Then just get out of the house and come stay with me."

"That's what Truck said."

Bam. Carrie felt the words right down to her gut. *Come stay with me.* The words any woman would kill to hear. But he'd said them to Jeannie as a friend, just as a friend...

She took a minute to regain her equilibrium. "Of course, he'd say that. That's what a friend would say."

"He's been great. I've leaned on Truck for years, he knows the whole story, and he's been saying for years that it's time for me to kick Eddie out and take over."

What could she say? "Maybe it *is* time."

"Yeah." Jeannie still didn't sound so sure. She opened the menu. "I think I want a steak. I think I want to chew him up and spit him out." She looked up at Carrie. "And you know what? Any sexy lady worth her salt knows just how to do it."

NOTHING HAPPENED with Jeannie between that dinner and the weekend they went down to Hunter Cove for the art show.

By then, the first of the trilake promotional pieces had been printed and were in Carrie's hands, and she was going to distribute them through the Hunter Cove Chamber of Commerce, which had a table at the show.

The booths lined Main Street so that the only parking was down the long side streets or the lots behind the stores. And it was crowded. Hunter Cove wasn't as far for Bostonites to drive as Bar Harbor, for example, and a juried art show drew not only art lovers but also collectors from away who hoped to discover the next trendy artist. It was a one-day affair, which made getting there even more critical for those serious buyers.

All day long, the judges went from booth to booth anonymously, viewing the works.

There were potters there, too, and jewelers, and water-colorists and quilters who sewed painterly scenes.

Carrie dropped off trilake brochures at the Chamber of Commerce table, chatted for a moment with the president of the chamber who would be manning the booth for most of the day, and then she and Jeannie began strolling around.

There were a hundred artists displayed, most of them local, and some from away. They viewed landscapes, seascapes, portraits, modern and surrealistic art, watercolors, pottery and quilts.

They found Callie, who was chatting with a neighbor, and Carrie bought one of her primitive prints.

They bought hot dogs, sodas and ice cream as they wandered through the stalls.

"This is a really good turnout," Carrie said thoughtfully, "but I wonder if they couldn't be doing a better job advertising it."

"You are looking for job opportunities everywhere," Jeannie said.

"I guess I am. The question is, do they want to expand the event, make it important and attract up-and-coming artists or do they want to keep it small? Either way, they could probably make it better known. I think I'll speak to the chamber president when I get a chance. There might be something here."

"How do you come up with ideas, just like that?" Jeannie said wistfully as she snapped her fingers.

"I don't know. I just do," Carrie said with a shrug, wishing that Jeannie would use more initiative, learn not to take no for an answer, and stop feeling so helpless. The problem with Jeannie was, she was too used to things being as they were. She hadn't done a thing about Eddie, August was almost at an end, and eventually she was going to have to tell him about the real estate courses, ask questions about the books and make some demands.

But Jeannie was still lacking in confidence and hadn't cultivated the ability to make possibilities out of nothing; her sexy-lady persona and her signing up for a course were about as audacious as she'd been in all the years Carrie had known her.

Carrie wondered whether her own tenacious follow-through on her own ideas didn't scare Jeannie just a little. Maybe, she thought, she should just take it down a notch. Jeannie didn't have to be privy to everything she was doing or planning. Or every job possibility she hoped to conjure up.

"Look at this," Carrie said, stopping abruptly in front of a booth in which was displayed a large unframed watercolor of ice skaters on a pond.

"Doesn't that look like the pond?" She peered at the price that was discreetly tacked on the wall beside it. Seventy-five dollars. Junie de Longo could frame it for her.

"Look at the trees, the way they ring the water. And that red roof in the distance. That could be straight across the pond from me. I like this. I think I'm going to buy it."

Trying to distract Jeannie with the painting didn't work. Jeannie saw exactly what she was doing, what Carrie wasn't admitting she was doing: she was feathering her nest, and she'd already started by painting the two rooms she lived in most, and she was adding accessories. New sheets and comforters, books, a bowl.

A painting.

It was beginning to look as if she planned to stay.

No. She just wanted to be comfortable for the time she would be there. That was all.

The only thing was, her decisiveness, her fearlessness was making Jeannie uncomfortable. How must Jeannie feel, watching her go after what she wanted and in some measure getting it?

"Watching you is an education," Jeannie said suddenly. "You go out and conquer the world, and I hide behind the walls of a bank. What have I done in the past two months?"

"Now, Jeannie—" Damn it, she knew it: Jeannie was feeling diminished by her aggressiveness.

"I got uplift," Jeannie said dolefully.

"There's something to be said for uplift," Carrie stated before Jeannie could get down on herself. "You have a whole new attitude. You're starting to take charge of your life. And you made a decision about a new direction."

"All fine and good," Jeannie said, her forehead creased with determination. "But uplift just isn't enough. I've been watching you, Carrie, and how you've taken a demoralizing situation and made something of it. You haven't hunkered down and put on blinders..."

Oh yes I have, Carrie thought, about some things...

"In spite of all your feelings, you've gone forward. Even if it's temporary, you've moved from the point where you were when you arrived to a place where you've made some semblance of a life for yourself. That's an important lesson for me, Carrie."

"Don't give me too much credit," Carrie said warningly. "Whatever you think, I'm just as scared and weak-willed as the next person."

"Well, even if that's true, your example has helped me come to the conclusion that I've been avoiding my issues for far too long. And I have to face my demon. It's time for me to confront Eddie. It's time for *me* to make a change."

Sometimes all you had to do was ask.

Carrie sat with her arms propped on her knees contemplating the pile of papers on her coffee table that represented the Hunter Cove Arts Council's thinking about the expansion of the art show. With it, there were impact studies on the prospective increase in traffic and effect on Main Street businesses. This was big, she thought, even for such a small town. And they wanted to make it bigger. They wanted it to rival the Portland Art Show.

She needed to do some real critical thinking on how to increase the perception of its importance. She could start by designing a signature logo and conceptualizing more prestigious-looking trophies. And they should pare down the prize categories and increase the monetary award, because what was most wanted should be hardest to get. That was good. And then she—and the council—would have to line up more distinguished sponsors. So a killer solicitation letter was on the list of preliminary things to do.

She made copious notes. And then she looked at the time. Ten o'clock.

Only ten o'clock. The nights were getting longer, she was sure of it, and she could not invent enough work to fill the empty hours.

But that was her decision. She'd choose work and being

alone over a relationship and misery any day. She'd done the
right thing by staying away from Truck.

But whether she'd done the right thing by Jeannie was an-
other story altogether.

The living room by then was too warm. She had a fire
banked in the stove, one of those new skills she had
learned since coming home, but she was feeling more
and more restless and edgy as the night wore on.

Carrie shrugged her arms into the sweater she'd
draped over her shoulders, and went out onto the porch.
It was cool out there; the temperature sometimes went
down into the forties late at night. From where she sat,
leaning against the railing just by the top step, the inside
of her house looked so warm and cozy. She had leaned
the watercolor against the back of the couch and the vi-
brant colors popped out right through the window. It
made that whole corner of the room seem welcoming
and lived in, and a place she wanted to be.

She couldn't believe that five months ago, she'd been
tortured by guilt and failure, on the run from rejection,
an illusory relationship and betrayal.

And now she was just on the run from Truck. But she had
the feeling she could never outrun him.

"It's not that easy."

She jumped as Truck's voice came at her out of the
dark. Was he psychic or something? How did he know
what she was thinking?

"Sure it is," she said with more nonchalance than she
felt.

He loomed up just below the porch steps. "Mind if I
come up?"

Her heart pounded wildly. She minded everything
about him. "I guess not."

He settled himself on the step next to her. "Did you really think it was a far, far better thing you did that night you sent me away?''

''I thought so.''

''Well, it's not going to work.''

''It's working,'' she said.

''Really? When your voice is shaking. Your hands are shaking. You mean to tell me that if I went over there and kissed you, you'd push me away?''

She wished he would, Carrie thought. Two weeks was too long, even if it was the smartest decision she'd made since she'd left New York. And her feelings were still so intense, she could almost feel his lips on hers. ''Yes. No. I don't know.''

''So where were we?'' he asked lazily.

''Stopping this.''

''But we don't want to stop it, do we, Carrie?''

''Yeah, we do.''

''Why is that?''

''It's not smart. We can't slow-dance in the dark forever.''

''So let's don't, Carrie. Let's slow-dance into the light.''

She turned her head away, feeling agitated, cornered. Truck shouldn't have come. ''That's not an option.''

''It sounds like a plan to me.''

''It's not a plan,'' Carrie said sharply. ''It's a trap.''

Snap! Vulnerable Carrie, scared silly that she'd permanently deadfall into someone's arms. He should have seen it, Truck thought. He shouldn't have given her a choice or a chance after that first kiss. And he'd made it too easy for her by playing her *phantom lover.*

''Exactly what pitfalls are we talking about, Carrie?''

She clenched her fists. ''Bad decisions. Mistakes. Illusions. Choosing the wrong person. And that's just at the top of my list," she said, her voice trembling.

"So what's the point?"

Her tension was palpable. "I *never* want to get stuck," she said fiercely. "Nothing is worth it. *Nothing*. Not a career, not great sex, not money, power, prestige. *Nothing*."

Truck silently took that in. He couldn't bear to hear her anguish, her hurt. It was so misguided, and it wasn't even the fearless, indomitable Carrie Spencer talking.

It was a child.

"Why?" he asked finally. "Why, Carrie?"

"Why? Why. Well, shall I confess all my sins to you, Truck? Shall I lean on you, the way Jeannie does?" *Mean thing to say, mean*, she thought instantly, remorsefully.

But she didn't care. She didn't. She was stronger than that, she always had been. And she could be strong about him too. She didn't need him. She didn't need anybody.

And that was the biggest illusion of all.

"I don't think so. It's hard enough to live with my own stupid mistakes, let alone share them with someone who can use them against me."

"Tell me why, Carrie."

"You probably know. Everybody knows. That's what Henry Longford tells me." She felt close to tears then.

"Yeah, they probably do," Truck agreed. "Why?"

"I promised my mother I'd never get into trouble," Carrie whispered.

"And I guess you didn't," he said finally because he didn't know where she was headed with it.

"You're damn right. Not with you, not with anyone. I swore I wasn't going to have her life. I wasn't going to be stuck raising a child on no money at all or constrained

from doing anything I wanted to by stupidly giving myself to some idiot who was thinking solely with his hormones. And I was that close to doing it with you, Truck.
I was closer than that, fifteen years ago. And then I saw
that house up the road and I had a vision of myself with
two babies hanging on to my jeans and 3:00 a.m. feed-
ings and housework and laundry, and that's when I
said—goodbye.''

"Okay," he said slowly. Just what she'd told him all
those years ago. No marriage and motherhood for her.
But he hadn't wanted that either. He'd just wanted her.

"When I was thirteen years old," Carrie said, her
voice quivering a little, "and starting to sneak down to
the boys' summer camp, Momma sat me down on that
rock down there, and she told me some home truths—
that some boy had gotten her pregnant, that he'd abandoned her. That her parents had thrown her out. That
she had always been all alone.

"She spent the rest of her life taking care of me, providing for me, making a home for *me*. And you know
what—nobody asked her what *she* wanted. *I* never
asked her what she wanted. I don't *know* what she
wanted."

Oh God, the words almost killed her; she'd never said
them out loud, she'd never even allowed herself to think
about them.

She went on in a rush: "But I thought I was hot stuff,
that everything revolved around what *I* wanted, what I
had to have. And when *I* had to leave, you know what
she did? Do you know?"

She looked at him with tears shimmering in her eyes.
"She let me go."

"That's what parents do, Carrie."

"Yeah, well. The only thing she ever asked of me was

to keep out of trouble, and keep out of strange guys' beds."

"Well, you were good at that, fifteen years ago," Truck murmured. "Obviously something changed."

"Chalk it up to another stupid mistake," Carrie said. "We never should have started."

"We haven't nearly finished."

"Oh yes, we have."

He moved close to her. Carrie couldn't back off, she couldn't back down. And there was so much heat already, from her confession, from her conflicted emotions, she wasn't sure she wanted to.

"You're hiding behind a crumbling wall, Carrie. And the truth of the matter is, your mother didn't have to be alone and lonely."

"What do you mean?" she whispered. "She was alone all her life."

"I mean, there was a lonely widower up the road from her who would have readily, gladly lifted her burden, given her companionship, and love, and eased her pain..."

"No..." She shook her head.

"Yes. *Yes.* My father could have loved her. Hell, he *needed* to love her. And you know what she said, Carrie? Every single word you've said, exactly the same."

"No. I don't believe you. It's too convenient. No."

"Everyone knew."

She felt that awful caving feeling inside. There was no escape from anything, even your past, because *everyone knew.* "I don't believe it."

"Ask Old Man."

I knew your mother, he'd said. Old Man, with whom she'd fallen instantly in love. Oh God, oh God, oh God.

She pulled her wits together. "Fine. What's your point?"

"Think about it—two people desperately needing someone to love, living five hundred yards apart and millions of miles away. You understand exactly what my point is. And nothing is going to make it go away."

"It has nothing to do with us."

"Your mother was very beautiful, Carrie, very sweet, so vulnerable. I remember her from the time when Old Man was trying to court her."

I never knew. I never ever knew...

"And she said no. No, she couldn't take the risk. No, she couldn't let go. Old Man could have been your step-father. He could have given you security and family and love. And what did your mother do? What *did* she do when she was offered a chance at love and commitment? I'll tell you, Carrie. *I'll* tell you. She hid."

"No...!"

"She *hid*..."

"She had reasons," Carrie snapped.

"She had no reason on earth," Truck said as he carefully moved closer, "to deprive you, Old Man, herself, me, of family, security, love and commitment." And closer. "And neither..." Closer. "...do..." He grasped her shoulders. "...you—"

"Don't." Her voice was stark, white-hot with contained fury. *"Don't."* She wrenched away from him. "You've said enough."

"I haven't said nearly enough," he said huskily. "You know what you've been doing the last two months?"

"I know damn well what I've been doing. I've been sleeping with you."

"You've been hiding."

"In plain sight," she retorted. "Nothing was hidden from you."

"Everything is hidden—in the dark."

The words hung between them. And it was so easy to give everything, she thought, in the dark.

She pushed at him blindly. "Go away."

He wrapped his arms around her, containing her surging body.

"I can't," she said stonily.

"You will."

"Leave it alone." She couldn't move. She wanted to run from him as fast and far as she could, and she wanted to stay right where she was forever. "You got what you wanted. So just leave me alone." She made a move to pull away from him.

"You don't have an idea in hell what I want," he growled, drawing her back and enfolding her against his strength and his heat. "Carrie—"

There was such raw need in his voice, in his tone, in the way he surrounded her and held her that she didn't know how she could ever have the strength to deny him anything ever again.

The phone rang, sharply, insistently.

"Don't answer it," Truck murmured. He had her; he really had her and they were on the edge of something deep and profound, and he wasn't going to let her go for anything.

But she felt the familiar tense excitement; she couldn't stand not to answer it, and she eased free of Truck's arms and darted into the house, while he followed angrily.

"Carrie, it's me, Jeannie. Listen, I'm with Old Man. I had it out tonight with Eddie, and I left him. He's so furious..."

"Whoa, Jeannie, whoa—" Carrie shook her head to try to take in what Jeannie was saying. But it was too far a step from the emotion of Truck's revelations to Jeannie's overwrought announcement.

She motioned to Truck. "It's Jeannie. She says she's at your house—" She held up the phone between them so he could hear what Jeannie was saying as well.

"Jeannie, did I hear you say you *left* Eddie? What happened?"

"I had it out with him, Carrie, and now I don't know what he's going to do. He wouldn't listen to me, he wouldn't listen to reason...and worst of all, he's blaming it all on you..."

This, on top of everything else. Carrie put the phone down slowly, her expression stricken. "I did this. Eddie's right. I'm the catalyst... If I hadn't come back, if I hadn't—"

She got no further; Truck buried her face against his chest, murmuring, "Don't, Carrie. Don't do that to yourself. It's been coming on for years, don't...don't... We all told her—don't—"

She cried. She didn't know whether she was crying for Jeannie or for herself, or her mother, but she cried, and Truck held her and smoothed her hair, and she couldn't stop. It all welled up from someplace she wasn't even aware of, all the anguish, all the lost opportunities, all her sorrow over the failure of Jeannie's marriage, all her conflicted emotions about Truck.

But she couldn't allow herself the luxury of tears, not for long. She pulled away from Truck and went to the kitchen to splash cold water on her face.

"Come on, we'll go up to my house," Truck said.

Which was exactly what she needed to do.

But, after all that emotion, and all that pain, Carrie felt

very strange walking into Old Man's house in the dead of the night, because she would be seeing it with new eyes and, after the evening's home truths, she didn't want to know what it was like, what she could have had, what she had missed.

It was a big comfortable house with an enclosed porch, a spacious living room with shelves and shelves of books, magazines, music, games, cushiony chairs and couches, tables of several heights and lamps conveniently placed for reading.

"So, Carrie," Old Man said, "you've finally come." *Home.* It hung in the air even though he didn't say it.

"I'm worried about Jeannie," she said.

"She'll be fine," he said reassuringly. "We've called our lawyer. We'll get an injunction. It looks worse than it is."

"But Eddie said—he asked me what kind of voodoo I was working on Jeannie."

"No law against that," Old Man said. "Sit down, Carrie. You look wiped out."

"Yeah, I am." She sank onto the couch. Jeannie was in the kitchen, conferring with Truck, who was on the phone.

They didn't need her here, she thought. And Eddie wasn't going to do anything drastic, like come after her. He was all bluff and bluster, he always had been. But he'd scared Jeannie to death. And there was that part of him that always seemed to be a little bit out of control. And now that Jeannie had, to all intents and purposes, taken everything away from him, what wouldn't he do?

"Jeannie's going to stay here," Old Man said. "You're welcome to stay too, Carrie, until this shakes out."

"Or I'll stay with her," Truck said, coming back into the room. "In fact, that might be the best solution."

"I wouldn't mind if someone asked me," Carrie put in irritably.

"You've already proven you're in no shape to make a coherent decision," Truck said. "I think we should all stay here tonight, and see what happens in the morning."

Jeannie made coffee, and they huddled around the game table in the far corner of the living room.

"I don't know where I got the nerve," Jeannie said, holding her cup tightly in her hands. "I think it was watching Carrie just steam ahead, making things happen in places you'd think there weren't any opportunities.

"I thought, I've been wasting opportunities. All the nights I wait up for Eddie. All the days I just get through, waiting for something to happen. And nothing ever does. Everything is the same. We're roommates, Eddie and I. I'm a piece of furniture. I'm something he put in his house to enhance his comfort.

"So when I started looking different, I threw him off balance. It was like I'd changed the furniture without asking him, and he suddenly didn't know where things were. He couldn't use them in the same way, because they were different and he wasn't used to it.

"He really liked Jeannie the farm woman. I was a glowing advertisement for the benefits of rural living. A woman on the farm is not one who spends a lot of money on *female* things, you know. And there's a certain kind of man that's really attracted to that idea.

"So, I started by buying new clothes, and you saw what happened at the dance. He was baffled. I was the same, and I was different in a way that I stood out suddenly. We fought a lot about that. He really wanted me to be like his mother. To be the person who created his comfort zone, and not question anything he ever did.

"And I did that for a long time. And when we didn't have babies, well, I made another comfort zone—for him. He didn't want to adopt. He wanted *his* kids or no kids."

"That must have been so hard for you," Carrie murmured, reaching out and grasping Jeannie's hand. "That was so mean. So thoughtless."

"Well, it's over," Jeannie said. "I finally found some attitude, some backbone. I found that men liked me just as I am now and that Eddie isn't the be-all and end-all in my life. But that was what I thought. I thought no one else could ever love me." Her voice crumpled. "The sad part is, he never really did."

Her eyes brimming with tears, Carrie looked up at Truck as if to say, *You see? You see?*

"You loved him for a long time," Truck said. "You tried." He looked right into Carrie's teary eyes. "It would have been sadder if you'd never tried."

They all managed to get a little sleep; Jeannie took the guest room, and Carrie curled up on the couch. In the morning, Truck took her back home so she could change, and she refused his offer to take her into town.

How dangerous could Eddie be? He was volatile but he wasn't stupid. Jeannie would go to work as usual and the lawyer would take care of the matter.

Nothing was going to happen.

Carrie was disabused of that notion very fast when she found the tires on her cycle viciously slashed that afternoon after she'd finished up at Longford's. It couldn't be ignored: Eddie meant business. He was coming after those he felt were responsible for uprooting his comfortable life.

He was coming after *her.*

TRUCK TOOK HER HOME. It was the last thing Carrie wanted, but he'd been the first person Henry Longford had called.

"Well, I told him to call me in case of trouble," Truck said, tuning out her tirade. "Just be quiet."

"I don't need you," Carrie said through gritted teeth. "I can deal with this on my own."

"Well, hell, I need you, and if Eddie Gerardo's turned into an ax murderer, I don't want to be the last to know. Just cool it, Carrie, until we make sure everything's okay at the house."

"You think he knows Jeannie's staying with you?"

"He probably thinks she's with you."

Uh oh. For the first time, Carrie felt a little frisson of fear.

"She didn't go to work today, by the way."

Worse and worse...and she'd left early: seven-thirty. It was almost two-thirty in the afternoon now.

Truck eased his van down the dirt track and came to a jolting halt.

Someone—Eddie—had been there.

Carrie sat there frozen, unable to grasp the scope of the wanton destruction. He had broken all the windows in the front of the house. He'd chopped up all the porch furniture, her makeshift desk, the birdfeeder hanging on a nearby tree. He'd dumped the plants she'd had hanging from the eaves of the porch, and shoveled manure all over the floor. And he'd cut the phone line.

Truck paged his father. A minute later, his cell phone rang.

"Carrie's place is a mess. I need Alden over here for emergency window repair, standard cottage double hungs—twelve sheets. And the sheriff. I can handle the rest. Yeah, I think it was Eddie. And someone slashed her tires." He flicked off the phone. "Old Man's got a cb. He'll catch the sheriff quicker wherever he is. We can't do anything until he comes anyway."

But he thought of ten violent things he wanted to do, all of them centering around the primitive urge to beat the hell out of Eddie Gerardo, and rub his nose in the muck on Carrie's porch.

She hadn't said a word. What was there to say? They all misjudged the depth of Eddie's resentment and fury. And he'd picked the most convenient target today. Who was to say tomorrow he wouldn't find and attack Jeannie?

She felt sick. Ill. Violated. There were no words for that.

She pushed herself to get out of the van just as the man from Alden's came strolling down the track.

"I think we're going to have to carry the glass down piecemeal," he said to Truck.

"So we'll carry it," Truck said as the sheriff's car drew up and he got out.

"Brad."

"Hey, Truck. This is something. Know who did it?"

"We think so, but there's no hard evidence."

"All right. Tell me what you know, we'll take some pictures and get on it from there."

Truck gave the sheriff the details and walked him over to the van where Carrie was standing. "Carrie, this is Sheriff Brad Hillis."

Carrie shook herself. Another face from the past, another one-two picture flashing in her mind, the young face superimposed on the older one.

"I remember you," she said.

"Sorry about this." He turned to Truck. "You think Old Man would mind if I dropped by and talked to Jeannie?"

"He probably expects you."

"Okay. I'll get a couple of pictures, and then you can clean up."

While he did that, Truck and the glazier brought down some of the fragile panes of glass and leaned them against the side of the porch.

Then Truck tackled the cleanup in earnest, a knight-errant to Carrie's benumbed princess until she could safely enter the castle.

Truck was right behind her. "He didn't get as far as transgressing in here obviously."

"He could've." She walked into the kitchen. "He could have been in every room. He could have *touched* things. I feel as if everything is tainted."

"Only if you let it..." Truck reached for her. "Only if you give him that power..."

Carrie clenched her fists. *The bastard.*

It would be so easy to let herself wallow in shock and let Truck pick up the pieces. And that was the last thing she wanted him to do.

"Don't let him in your house, Carrie." His voice was soft in her ear, his arm sliding around her unobtrusively, and instinctively she leaned against him. Just for a moment. Just for one small solid reassuring minute, she let him comfort her. "Don't let him in your life."

She felt so secure when he held her, so safe. And she felt the danger from him, too.

If she gave in, if she let Truck do everything, if she let him in her life, he would have the power...and she would have...?

Love? Commitment? Family?

She didn't want to go there.

The only antidote was action. She pulled away from him abruptly, grabbed a broom and some garbage bags and, without a word, she went outside.

she won't need to go there.

The only trouble was that if she pulled away from him sexually, she pulled away in *other ways*, too. She'd probably once a week, maybe, if

11

IT TOOK ALL DAY and into the evening for the windows to be replaced and to scrub the stench of manure from the floorboards of the porch. Everything else they'd piled in a heap at the side of the house to be loaded into a small Dumpster that would be delivered tomorrow. By that time, it was almost nine o'clock. Alden's men had finally left and Carrie was foraging for something to eat. Not that she was hungry but Truck surely had to be; all he'd had was four cups of coffee in the interim.

"I can make you a fast pasta," she offered.

"Don't rush on my account."

She prickled instantly. "Oh yeah? What does that mean?"

"It means I'm not going anywhere. And I'm especially not going anywhere if you're staying here."

Carrie slammed the pantry door. "I just lost my appetite."

"And I'm ravenous."

Carrie stamped out of the room. He had a hell of a nerve, she fumed, assuming...things...just because they'd worked so efficiently together all day.

She stood on the porch and rubbed her hands over her face. What a day!

Jeannie had come over in the late afternoon to see what Eddie had done and she'd been horrified.

"He thought you were here," Truck had told her. "He

probably thought he'd fix you *and* Carrie but good. But look, Brad's handling it now. And the lawyer. So you just stay with Old Man until things clear up."

"But what about Carrie? What about you?"

"Jeannie...don't be naive."

Her mouth had rounded. "Oh. *Oh...*"

Although Jeannie had insisted that she wanted to stay and help, both Carrie and Truck had insisted that they had things under control and it would be best for Jeannie to go back to Truck's. Reluctantly, Jeannie had agreed.

Were it so easy to convince Truck that she could take care of herself. But Truck wasn't going anywhere. He had followed her out to the porch. "I don't need a nursemaid," she hissed, throwing up her hands.

"Fine." Truck squared off in front of her. "Throw me out."

"You're not going to convince me of anything by staying, you know," she said.

"I wouldn't bet on it," he murmured.

There was nothing he could say or do, she was immune to him now, Carrie thought. And all the things he'd told her last night washed every other feeling away.

Carrie strode past, and back inside the house. He wanted to stay, so let him! She was immune to him now, wasn't she?

Yet the intimacy of having him in the house was stunning. This was way different than his subtle sensual entrances and exits during their nights of phantom love. This was Truck, sitting in her living room, expanding the space, filling it to the point that she felt as if she were suffocating.

It became a contest of wills. Carrie wasn't going to bed

until he left. He wasn't leaving and she might just as
well go to bed.

Neither of them had to say a word. It was in the air.
Her temper. His determination. And shimmering under
that, a galvanic awareness of each other that hadn't diminished under the onslaught of revelations.

It was almost too much for her. She was spent, physi-
cally and emotionally. Nonetheless she was so keyed up
she thought she'd never sleep again.

"It's okay," he said at one point. "I'm not going anywhere."

"It's *not* okay. And stop saying things like that."

"Fine, but you'd better understand something. I'm
staying with you until this thing with Eddie is cleared
up. And even then I may never go home."

She let out her breath in a huff. "I didn't hear that."

"I haven't spared you anything, Carrie. You've *gotten*
everything."

I haven't gotten you out of my system, she thought. As
much as she kept telling herself she was immune to
Truck, the heat between them was still there.

She bolted out of her chair. "I'm going to bed."

But it wasn't any easier blocking out his presence
when she couldn't see him, because he was so aggres-
sively *there,* and he was still the phantom lover of her
dreams.

HE DROVE HER TO WORK, he brought her back home.

"Don't *you* have any work to do?"

"I delegated. Come on, Carrie. This isn't so terrible."

"When I get my cycle back..."

Well, he'd managed to delay that, at least. Dooley, the
Harley mechanic in Portland, had called to say they had
to order the tires. It would be a week, maybe less.

Carrie gritted her teeth. A week of him living with her. *Living with her!* After all her fuss about what people would think if he took her out to dinner. She couldn't believe it. He just wasn't going home. Period.

He made dinner for her the following evening.

She swallowed it down. This was too cozy, too intimate, too much like...like...she couldn't even think the words.

"Have the police seen any sign of Eddie?"

"No. He wasn't at the house, he never came in to the office. He's got a girl working there who's been fielding phone calls because he had a couple of contracts pending. But no closings, thank God."

Jeannie had taken some vacation time, confessing to Carrie over the phone that she hadn't had a vacation in years. "Eddie was always working, never wanted to go anywhere. Don't get me started. Being up here with Old Man is like being in a private resort where nobody bothers you and you can rest and relax to your heart's content."

And Jeannie did look less peaked, Carrie thought when she and Truck went up to Old Man's the following night for dinner. And if it weren't for the circumstances, it would be just like a Sunday-night family gathering.

What is happening here?

Jolley had made a big pot of stew, and Truck had picked up some French bread from Verity's, and fresh butter from the farm up on Hill Road. There was cider and lemonade and iced tea, and Jeannie had baked a carrot cake for dessert.

About a half hour into the meal, Brad Hillis dropped by to update them on the fact that Eddie was still missing. They invited him to dinner. And Tom appeared to see how Jeannie was getting on.

Suddenly it was a party. Old Man got out some music. They pulled away the tables and chairs. Tom and Jeannie started dancing. The whole thing caught Carrie by surprise.

"Come on, Carrie." Truck took her arm.

"Oh, no. No," she protested. "This is how the whole thing started."

"What thing?"

"The night thing. The slow-dancing thing."

"Carrie, it's only a dance. And damn, I know I've said that line before." He pulled her into his arms; she was stiff as a board. She wasn't getting any closer to the seductive movement of his body than she had to. She wasn't going to let anything happen between them ever again.

"Carrie, you are not a fool, and you are fooling yourself so badly, it's painful to watch."

"Then *don't*."

"Hell, I have a front-row seat," he muttered, "and I'm not giving it up to anybody."

Later still, they played some of the old board games that Old Man had stashed on the shelves, and finally near midnight, Truck took Carrie home.

"Don't you worry none, Miz Carrie," he drawled as they walked through the door of her house. "I'm right here to protect you."

She bit her tongue. Why start with him, when she'd had such a good time?

When had she enjoyed an evening out so much? She tried to picture pulling in the neighbors in her New York apartment building for an evening of music, games and talk. Not possible. They'd have filled their datebooks months in advance because there was no greater sin than not having somewhere to go and something to do.

She slammed the bedroom door. This whole body-guard business was getting on her nerves. There was a look in his eyes she did not like, and body language she did not trust.

You didn't turn off wants, needs and desires like a faucet. They bubbled just beneath the surface, potent and hot, and sometimes, when she looked at Truck, when she remembered...her body swelled, unfurling toward his heat, with the confidence he knew all her dark secrets and he was waiting for her.

It was exactly what she didn't want, she thought as she yanked off her clothes and got ready for bed. They were poised, all of them, waiting for something, some-one, or some explosive moment that would define the thing between them for once and for all.

CARRIE AND TRUCK WENT to see Old Man on Thursday night, normal stuff, real-life stuff. He and Jeannie were on the porch playing hearts.

There was nothing new. Old Man was certain Eddie had skipped the county. The house was empty, the office closed. The police couldn't do much else but issue an APB, but Brad Hillis was certain Eddie had gone into hiding somewhere in town.

"He could be waiting for Jeannie to return to the house," Old Man theorized. "For all we know, he's somewhere on the pond. He could be watching us now."

Carrie shivered. There were deep woods surrounding the pond. And the abandoned camp with no one to over-see it but a caretaker who walked the grounds daily but probably didn't go about at night.

"That was the first place Brad thought to look," Truck said. "There wasn't any sign of him."

"I'll make some coffee," Jeannie offered. Carrie followed her into the kitchen.

"This must be killing you," Carrie said, as she helped Jeannie wash the pot and the mugs.

"I thought it would be over by now," Jeannie said. "It's been almost a week since he trashed your place. I'm beginning to feel like I'm in jail." She got the coffee tin out of the refrigerator. "I think there's some leftover cookies or something in there. I'm really glad you came by. How's it going with Truck?"

"It's going. He won't leave, and I don't want him to stay."

"That's my Trucker. Stubborn as ever. How many cups should I make?"

"Is Tom going to—"

Blam! A gunshot reverberated through the woods, shattering glass. Jeannie shrieked.

"Get down!" Truck shouted from just outside the kitchen door.

Blam! They dived for the floor as the fixture above them exploded into a thousand pieces.

Blam! The bullet ricocheted off something in the kitchen. Close. Too close. Damn close.

And Old Man...?

"Put down your gun." They heard a metallic voice, speaking through a bullhorn, in the distance. "Put...down...the...gun."

Another shot fired nicked the window. And another, going off wildly and fracturing the roof just outside the kitchen door.

Shouts. More shots. A keening howl far away.

There was Truck crouching beside them in the kitchen. "It's Eddie. They've been waiting for him. I think they got him. Brad was right. He never went away."

THEY STAYED with Old Man that night, Carrie on the couch again, Jeannie in the guest room, weeping. Eddie, who had been wounded, had been taken to the hospital, and Brad Hillis took their statements, and asked Jeannie to come to the station in the morning.

"How can I ever go back home?" Jeannie asked tearfully.

"You can always go back home," Old Man said.

Truck drove them both into town in the morning, taking Carrie over to Longford's first before he and Jeannie went to the police station.

No one in town had yet heard about the ruckus, at least as much as Carrie could determine that morning. No one mentioned it, which surprised her. She thought the news about Eddie would have gone through town like wildfire.

Later that morning, however, she heard that Eddie might have to go away for long-term treatment.

By two o'clock, Carrie was really ready to go home. It wasn't that the day had been onerous. It was just that she felt edgy, fragile and needed to be home.

What she didn't need was Truck coming to pick her up.

"When did you say those tires would be coming in for my cycle?"

"Any day now," Truck said, depressing the power locks as she belted herself into the front seat of the van.

"I think it's time I got a car."

"Good idea."

"I think it's time you got a life," she added irritably.

"I have one, thank you, and I like it very much."

"You like your house getting shot up?"

"No. But I like you in my house," Truck retorted.

"Don't count on it," Carrie muttered. God, he was relentless. He just never gave up, and she swore she wouldn't let him wear her down. But he'd been getting mighty close to it these past couple of nights, and all because he had left her alone.

"Stop hiding, Carrie."

"What is this, your mantra?"

"No, it's *your* motto."

"I hate you."

"I'm still not leaving you tonight."

"Of course you are. You are *not* staying tonight."

"I am."

"Listen, you play a mean Kevin Costner but Eddie is history now and so are you."

"Burying your head in the sand, Carrie?"

"I'm not even going to talk to you."

"Hiding, Carrie."

"My lips are sealed," she muttered.

"Sensory deprivation."

"*Stop it!*"

"No, *you* did that, Carrie, all by yourself. To both of us. You sure you don't want to rescind it?"

"I'm sure I'm never getting in this van with you again," she said furiously.

"I wouldn't be so sure of anything if I were you," he murmured as he turned onto the Pond Road.

"You can let me off at the top of the road."

"No, I'd be a sorry bodyguard if I let you walk down that dirt road in your best clothes. Don't make it harder than it has to be."

Carrie made choking sound. "I'll forget you said that."

Truck jammed on the brakes. "I haven't forgotten a thing."

Me neither.

She stared at him, feeling that subversive little pin-prick of desire. There wasn't a pore in her body that didn't want to melt into his arms at this moment.

This thing between them was getting scarier and scarier. She didn't want to need him or want him, and she did—she did.

She couldn't.

She bolted out of the van before he cut the engine.

HE STILL HAD some finish work to complete under the house and in the bathroom. It was enough to keep him occupied until dinnertime, at which point he found Carrie in the kitchen frying chicken.

"You can have some, but I'd rather you went home to Old Man."

"That's funny. Old Man would prefer I stay here with you." He went into the bathroom to wash his hands, and Carrie felt a little curlicue of awareness slither through her. There was something about a man in the bathroom, and the way he lathered up his arms and face and...

Stop it!

Carrie made a salad and dished out the chicken and sat down across the counter from him. Too domestic. Too scary.

He was talking to Old Man on the cell phone. "Jean-nie's back there, a little shaken up. Eddie got a flesh wound last night, and they're putting him under psychi-atric evaluation. Jeannie told him she'll be filing the sep-aration papers this week."

Carrie had been expecting that news, but it shocked her all the same.

"And the business. They're going to make some arrangement for Jeannie to take over the business. She may close it down until she gets her real-estate license. She'll keep the house."

"Brad did a good job of keeping the details contained," Carrie said.

"Yes, he did. But some of it will come out. It won't hurt Jeannie though."

"Well, she's in pain now," Carrie said pointedly.

"It's a terrible thing, to be in love, to risk loving, and then to have everything fall apart. You're right, Carrie. It's better to just keep your distance. It's better to withdraw. Hibernate. It's better to be alone and lonely."

She jacked herself away from the counter. "You do *not* have all the answers."

"You don't understand, Carrie. I *am* the answer."

That sent her storming from the house. Without a jacket, and into the cold night air. She heard him in the dark behind her, gathering twigs and branches to feed the fire in the stove, the hunter providing for his mate.

She had to stop thinking like this.

Truck thought he was so wily, giving her time, giving her the latitude to come to terms with her fierce need for independence and her ferocious need for him.

But Carrie had tamed that overwhelming desire. And it was a tightrope walk. The failure of Jeannie's marriage had nothing to do with her. She had always known that, really. But she infinitely preferred the idea of the phantom lover to a relationship that would pervade all areas of her life.

Her life was fine right now, thank you. She was content with the little space she'd made for herself here. She liked the tempo, the work, the people. She liked the town, and reconnecting with Jeannie.

She didn't need promises, guarantees, happy-ever-afters.

But she needed something.

I need a phantom lover...

Instantly, she banished the thought. That way was trouble. She would have become dependent on it, she would have craved more.

Well, guess what, Carrie. You do want more. You've just been submerging that need the way you always do when things get too close to the bone.

No, she thought. It hadn't gotten that far with Truck.

It's better to be alone and lonely...

She felt a nascent ache rising right from the center of her body, and she shivered. Her mother had died, alone and lonely, while Old Man waited patiently down the road.

I am the answer...

Actually, I thought it was love...

THEN SOMETIME in the night, Carrie awakened, her body prickling to be touched, to be stroked, to be filled. She clamped down on the feeling ruthlessly. But it had a life of its own. It billowed inside her, insistent, vital, erotic, *necessary.*

And no phantom lover to assuage the need...

Maybe—

She slipped out from under the cozy warmth of her down comforter. It was dead cold in the room, cold enough to bank the most sensual fire. And she needed that to cool her heated body, her burning imagination.

She needed...warmth...

She wrapped herself in her robe and opened the bedroom door.

Truck stood on the threshold, one arm braced against the door frame, his heat, his desire almost palpable.

Her body turned liquid. *She wanted...*

Everything.

And she knew what that meant. She understood the cost, because he would take nothing less now.

In his eyes, she read... *All or nothing. You take me, you take the phantom, you take the man.*

"Yes or no, Carrie?" His voice was hoarse, barely above a breath as he gave her the choice.

Truck knew so much about her. He knew everything. He had never been her phantom lover. He had always been real. She was the one who lived in a fantasy.

But this—if she said yes—he would make this real and nourish it in the sun, this ache, this need...

"Yes," she whispered. *Yes...*

Yes...

His mouth over hers, testing hers, sinking into hers. This, this she had yearned for. On and on as they moved into the warmth of the outer room, and sank onto the floor, his kisses lush, wet, enfolding, arousing.

Kiss me forever, don't do one other thing—

His urgent hands stroking her, his heat enveloping her soft bare skin.

Truck was a man who couldn't wait. He took her hands and raised them over her head, and he drove into her with a voracious hunger.

Him, him, it was all him, his hot elemental force pinning her to the floor in primal rhythm as old as the sun. Hot as the sun. Her sun, her center, convulsing her, fracturing her with the incandescent light of completion.

He soared beside her, a mythic hero with melting wings. And then he fell through the incendiary heat and back down to earth.

EVERYTHING CHANGED.

This was what it was like, having a full-time lover, who came home and couldn't wait to take you to bed, who loved you in the morning, at night, sometimes even during the day.

Carrie was busy, so busy. The Hunter Cove Arts Council drive to expand its show had heated up. The Trilakes Committee decided it wanted a bigger promotional piece, maybe a magazine like the state of Massachussetts had been publishing every summer.

She continued to do the ads for Longford's, to manage the office and mind the store.

And over and above that, she was having fun. She and Truck went everywhere, from dinner out, to the fall stock-car races and the annual county fair.

They went out with Jeannie, Tom, Brad Hillis and his wife. Or they all came over to visit Old Man.

Eddie was gone, having paid his fines in lieu of days served, and signed all the separation and division-of-property papers, having agreed to a quick divorce.

Jeannie had started the real estate courses at night school.

The weather was cooling down appreciably, the leaves falling, and tourists were bussing all over New England to get a taste of fall.

There was something so cozy about just lying naked with your lover under a warm down cover on a lazy Friday afternoon.

My lover, real and all there...

Amazing how being with him, wanting him, made her aroused all over again. Once a day sometimes just wasn't enough.

Lying in her bed together in the late afternoon of a

crisp quiet autumn day, Carrie felt his hands on her breasts, feeling them in just that way.

Yes. She started to boil. There was something about the movement of his hands, *that* way... She stretched languidly, like a cat, the ripple of her body issuing an invitation no man could mistake.

He cupped her body against him, covering her breasts with one hand and sliding the other downward between her legs. And he held her there, tightly and purposefully, his mouth at her ear.

"Ready?" A breath of a question.

"Almost—"

"What about now?" as he moved both hands to stroke her.

"I could be..."

"And now...?" Pressing her, demanding some response.

She caught her breath, her hips surged toward his expert fingers—

And the phone rang.

"Don't answer it."

"No."

Insistent.

"Let the machine." His tongue flicked against her ear.

This is Carrie Spencer. Leave your message after the tone...

"Carrie? Carrie?" An urgent voice, one she recognized instantly. She pushed Truck's hand away, and levered up on one elbow to listen. "Carrie, listen. Something big is coming up. International client. New image. Big money. I need you yesterday, even on a freelance basis. We'll pay all expenses, and more. Call me."

Carrie drew in a deep shuddery breath. "Oh my God. Oh...my...God—"

"So who exactly was that?" Truck sat up and looked over at her.

I have to compose myself. I have to get a grip.

She blew out a breath. "That was Elliott, my former partner in crime at the agency. I guess...I guess they need some help."

It wasn't so simple suddenly. She was thinking she could fly to Boston and shuttle to New York. Meet with Elliott. See where she would go from there. The first contact didn't necessarily mean she had the job. But oh, she felt more charged up than she had in months.

Truck knew it too. He watched it happen, watched her shut him right out and jettison everything they'd shared in the past three months because she'd made her decision even before Elliott stopped speaking, and she never even thought about talking it over with *him*.

"You're going," he said flatly.

"I have to." No hesitation. No consideration. No thinking about it, even. It was almost as if she had been waiting for this—the call to vindication, absolution, and the resurrection of her dreams.

Truck wondered what he'd expected: that the power of his love, his determination, and their connected past would bind her to him forever?

The warrior princess never quit, and he, better than anyone, should have known that. He should have been more aware that the siren lure of New York had always been in the air, and she'd never stopped listening for it.

"Truck—" She put out a conciliating hand, but she knew there was nothing she could say, nothing she could do. She had always known that someday she would have to leave him behind.

New York is calling.

And I have to go....

12

CARRIE SHRUGGED into her leather coat as Jeannie picked up her bags to load them into her car.

"You're crazy, you know that?"

"I have to go," Carrie said, and she meant it. She hadn't known how much she meant it until the call came. The mystical call.

"You're killing Truck."

"Yeah, well, he'll survive." There she was, the old Carrie, pushing everything aside, every consideration. Every want, need, desire. Every*one*. The career was the thing, the stepping stone to superstardom.

"Listen, you called this guy a weasel, Carrie. You said he was ruthless, a shark. What do you think he really wants?"

"You know," Carrie said as she locked up the house, "I actually thought about that. It isn't that he just snapped his fingers and I come running. This is a desperation move, he's pulling whoever he can from any quarter. So if I keep my head, and keep him out of my way, I have a chance to make my mark."

"But do you really want to?" Jeannie asked. "What's it going to get you in the long run?"

Carrie paused as she opened the car door. "I don't want to think about that just yet because I don't really know."

And maybe that was the most troubling question

about her decision to leave. She was throwing away too much for an indefinable gain.

Well, she thought, she'd deal with that later. And anyway, she'd done as much as she could here...at least for now.

Carrie shoved every feeling about Truck to the deep recesses of her mind. She knew how to do it, too. It was like focusing a bright beam of light straight ahead, and letting it fill your sightline so that everything else receded into shadow.

That was Truck, her phantom lover once more, creating enough memories to keep her warm for a lifetime.

He hadn't come to say goodbye.

Once Truck had understood her mind was made up, he'd gotten out of bed, had packed his few clothes and without another word, he'd left her.

And she hadn't even cried.

That told her something: that nothing in Paradise could hold her. And she'd always been ready to go.

THERE WAS NOTHING like New York in the early fall, with the cool crisp air, and everyone moving with a sense of purpose and always, it seemed, with someplace to go.

Carrie walked from her hotel, arranged for by the company, to the offices of Global Vision International located at Third Avenue and 52nd Street.

Nothing had changed. The lobby of the building was built top to bottom of marble.

When Carrie stepped into Global's familiar chrome-and-mirror reception area, she felt as if she was stepping back in time. She gave her name to the receptionist and settled herself in one of the cushy brown leather sofas that lined the mirrored walls.

Behind those walls was the creative department, an

open space where writers and artists worked together sharing ideas and opinions as they created award-winning ad campaigns.

And back there, in the corner office that had once been hers, Elliott was waiting for word she'd arrived.

His secretary came to get her.

She was pleasantly surprised by how many people waved to her, remembered her as they made their way through the maze of cubbyholes and desks.

"Carrie." Elliott came forward to meet her, his hand extended. Elliott hadn't changed either except that he was heavier. But he'd always been stocky with a professional air about him and a comfortable face, lined and lived in, that belied his sharp wit, intuition, off-the-wall humor and outrageous ideas. "God, I'm glad you're here. Come on in. Roxanne, get coffee."

"Right."

"Sit," he said, motioning her to a leather sofa in the far corner of the room. "This is great."

"Is it?" she asked curiously.

"Look, we were a great team. And I need teamwork for this project. This is huge. We've got a whole floor sectioned off and we're working in the utmost secrecy. I'm afraid you're going to have to sign a hundred papers pledging not to talk, but—" he waved his hand "—that's nothing compared to the prestige this account will bring if we win it. This is the first go-round to the golden ring. So, are you game?"

She'd gotten smarter, she thought. She couldn't be bowled over by Elliott's tactics anymore. She couldn't even see what she had ever loved in him. His quick mind? His golden tongue? He could sell ice to an Eskimo; and he'd sold her a bill of goods.

But not this time. "Let's talk money. I don't live here

anymore. How badly does Global want the account? What are they prepared to spend?"

"They want it, I want you, and we're both prepared to deal." He named a figure.

Carrie didn't blink. "That's nice. That's real nice. But I need a place to live, I need meals, I need transportation."

"They'll pay the full three months' rent in the residential hotel across the street. That encompasses the deadline, the due date and the end of round one. They've rented three floors in the Casa Suites. They want minimal outside contact. You'll get breakfast, lunch and dinner here. We're talking here about being totally sequestered until we come up with concept and campaign. Like sitting on a major trial. So?" He paused, and stared straight at her.

"Okay. You've got me."

"Great. This is really great. Guess what, you're going to work right now."

He grabbed the container of coffee from Roxanne's hand as they passed her out the door.

The war room was on the next floor. She had to be processed through a personnel office to get a badge, a key and ID. She had to sign papers that said she would forfeit her salary, her perks, and maybe even be prosecuted if she ever revealed the nature of the work going on behind those huge high walls.

What am I doing here?

"Oh good," Elliott said. "Breakfast is on."

Elliott brought her into the war room and introduced her around. She knew some of the faces, and some of the names, big names that had been brought in for recognition value and creative juice.

After that, she got the debriefing and pounds of corporate papers to study.

The floor had been sectioned off into offices surrounding an open space. Each writer-and-artist team was assigned one room in which they were set up with everything they would need from computers to fax machine, and of course, a coffeemaker. There was a common supply room, a library and three large conference rooms.

"And," Elliott said as he showed her around after breakfast, "I'm going to be your partner."

Carrie wondered why she wasn't surprised, and she found she was liking him less and less and she hadn't even been here three hours. What was it about him? He was running on nerves, she could tell that because she knew him so well, and he thought he was still trading on an affection that didn't exist anymore. She didn't care about him at all, and he thought, he hoped, she did.

No, she understood she was here for the recognition and the money, and it was clear to her that she was going to do hand-to-hand battle with the other heavyweights to get her due.

What the hell had she gotten herself into?

Still, the excitement of being back in New York was a heady sensation. And the adrenaline rush of beginning something new left no room for anything else. She had to focus every resource she had on the project.

That was good. That meant there was no time to think about Truck, to miss him, yearn for him or have regrets about might-have-beens.

IT REALLY WAS a full-immersion project. Every morning the hotel desk awakened her at six-thirty, as she'd instructed. She showered, she dressed, she was across the street at the office at eight for breakfast, at which point they were already working, and she usually was not back in the hotel until ten.

It was a ferociously difficult campaign for a client that was notoriously jittery about making the wrong move, a client that had the reputation of never taking its agency's advice. A client that was mired in its own inability to be decisive and was losing some major market share.

I'm tilting at windmills.

And Carrie didn't even feel like she was really in New York. The war room could have been in any building anywhere in the country. All she got of the city every day was the rush of traffic on 52nd Street on her way back to the hotel.

No Bloomingdale's. No theater. No concerts. No museums.

But then, those were intertwined with memories of Elliott: corporate seats at Madison Square Garden for the Knicks, the Rangers, the hottest Broadway shows, the best restaurants.

Elliott was the kind of guy who couldn't sit still and who always had to be seen.

There'd never been time for the small moments. A walk in the park. A steamy pretzel from a street vendor on a brisk fall day. A street fair in Brooklyn. The city on a Sunday—quiet, serene, and still full of an energy found nowhere else on earth.

Truck would like walking in the city, she thought, despite its size. He'd love the park, the dogs—*they* would have a dog, she thought—and sitting for hours with the *Times* on a Sunday...

They would have a what?

Dear Lord, was she so stir-crazy already that she was planning a life she never wanted?

But there was no time to analyze those too-frequent moments when Truck crept into her thoughts.

There was just time for pure, concentrated creative development. And time passing, rushing, fast.

CARRIE HAD BEEN GONE a month, Truck thought, and it felt like a lifetime. She'd written him short notes every few days which had devolved into E-mails, brief and frustratingly impersonal. *Client is difficult. Working round the clock. Off to try a new concept. Got to work up a new campaign.*

Truck couldn't understand work like that. Too nerveracking. He liked things he could touch, things he could put together, he liked problems he could solve and immediately see the result.

And he couldn't for the life of him solve the puzzle of why Carrie had gone.

Maybe it was one of those things: the past doomed to repeat itself. Maybe he would never understand.

"Go get her," Old Man kept telling him. "Maybe you shouldn't have let her go."

But how did you *keep* an independent spirit like Carrie when all the desire in the world was not enough?

And if he'd ever mentioned love, she would've left the first day back in town.

Love... He'd fallen faster than a summer storm the minute he saw her. But love wasn't in the vocabulary of the high flying, big-city woman Carrie had become.

And Elliott, who was just a deep raspy voice on a piece of tape still had had the power to move Carrie four hundred miles south while he, Truck, with all the intimacy they'd shared, didn't have the magic words to keep her in Paradise.

That said something potent about love and desire...and the foolishness of dreams.

Or had he just been hanging on until Carrie finally understood what she was fighting so hard.

He knew, but now wasn't the time to console himself with the words. Right now he had to find a way to just keep going.

So he worked on her house in the mindless numbing hours after work when there was nothing else to do. He retiled her bathroom, he rewired the electrical system. He thought about the winter, and how the heating system that Old Man had rigged for her mother wouldn't be even adequate after the previous year's storms, and how he could fix that problem.

"Come on, Truck," Jeannie egged him on, urging him to go out with her and Tom. Whenever he ran into Jeannie she looked proud, pretty and together, and Truck supposed that while she might never come to terms with her broken marriage, she had learned to be reasonably content with the outcome.

Jeannie was back in her house on the Pond, she was studying for her real estate license, and she was almost ready to jump-start her own business from the ruins of Eddie's real estate firm.

And Tom was definitely in the picture.

Sometimes a person's life did turn around, Truck thought. And then sometimes it just got turned upside down.

And it made a man understand: he'd been waiting for Carrie all these years, waiting for love.

And all for nothing. Carrie was gone, and with her, he'd lost another piece of himself.

ANOTHER FRUITFUL and fruitless day. Elliott caught up with Carrie as she exited the building. "How about we get a drink? There's a bar right in the hotel."

"Sure." Carrie let him guide her because she felt so weary.

The bar was right inside the door, and was crowded and noisy. They found a secluded corner, and Carrie sagged into the booth.

She didn't even know what she wanted. They were provided all day long with unlimited coffee, tea and soft drinks. Anything more potent was dangerous. She could sleep for a year.

She ordered juice and Elliott gave her a damping look. She knew what his objection was: a small glassful in this posh bar cost as much as a half gallon in the store.

Well, he ought to be made to pay. He hadn't half paid for all the anguish he'd caused her, and all the misery he was putting her through. She hated working with him. A partnership that had been so charged up six or eight months before was now a battle of wills that left her wrung out and angry every day.

So that was probably the reason for this little off-the-cuff meeting, where bosses couldn't eavesdrop, and everything they said would be between themselves.

"So...tell me," he began, "what *have* you been doing these past months you've been out of circulation?"

Spin time, she thought. You never told the truth. And you never quite lied. "Well, I went back home, I straightened out a few things, and then I started my own business. You know, you find those niches, and you grab the opportunities when they present themselves."

"No kidding. Clients?"

"I'm building slowly. Local stuff mainly. The arts council and the Trilakes Chamber of Commerce. About a dozen area businesses. Not million-dollar clients by any means, but enough to build a dream on." That was poetic, she thought. Did she mean it? And if she did, *why* was she here?

"Yet you accepted the offer to come back here."

Yes, he was getting at something. "It was short term enough so I could delegate my ongoing projects. And I wanted to get some seed money, and maybe a credit for my résumé. Big-name campaigns always help when you want to move up, don't they, Elliott?"

He smiled sourly. "We did work well together."

Did.

"But something's missing now, isn't it?"

She didn't know quite which way to play it. He was either going to fire her or assign her to someone else. And maybe better heads had prevailed on that decision.

Which did she want, in her heart of hearts?

"We do seem to have different ideas about the direction things should be going," she said carefully.

"We do. I'm glad you're thinking that way, and that we both want what's best for the client. I wonder whether you'd want to give it a shot with Andrea Lopez."

Her heart leaped. "Sure. I know Andrea."

"Good." He took a gulp of his drink. "I guess we weren't meant to be that dream team."

"I guess not," Carrie murmured. *I know not.*

And it was only the end of September.

Dear God.

Why am I here?

CARRIE SENT Truck a flurry of E-mails: *Things are heating up. I changed partners and now I can dance. Concept finalized. Prints and story on the boards. Competition cutthroat. Secrecy imperative. Cannot talk.*

It was as if she was working for some counterintelligence organization. You couldn't get hold of her, she was as formless as air.

And by the time Truck responded to her last message, her E-mail address had been encrypted and eliminated. It was as if she had vanished into a maw.

He didn't even try to figure out what she meant by those messages.

He just made sure the leaves were cleaned off of her roof and porch. He started to install an electric baseboard heating system. He worked on her computer, and slept at home.

October came. Passed. Weather got chillier and chillier. The tourists left, the woodpiles grew. Winter was coming on.

He tended to think like that now, in short, effortless phrases that required no energy and barely any communication.

"Go after her, son," Old Man kept telling him.

He had work to do, and no time at all to waste on chasing after a teenager's dream. But the dreams were still there, fueled by the blinking cursor of an E-mail message, a tenuous link at best, that brought New York that close to Paradise.

A man could always hope.

He took on a helper, and more installations than he could handle. Things always got real busy toward winter and it meant he didn't have to think too hard about the fact she was E-mailing him less and less. Because if he did, he didn't know what he would do, and it was all he could do to keep his feelings suppressed and his desire in check.

"Go after her," Jeannie kept telling him. "You don't understand. Carrie's really changed. She liked what was happening here. I think she loved you."

Go after her, after her, after her...
...actually, I thought it was love—

DECEMBER 15. Client meeting. Deadline. Panic.

Every agency pitching the account received a schedule of presentation. The end was almost near, and Carrie sat at her drawing board with Andrea Lopez over her shoulder, and studied her presentation.

This was the end. This was it. Whether they won or lost, she was gone. And she couldn't wait to be gone.

She had forgotten about the protocols and the layers of bureaucracy. She had forgotten about how fingers meddled in your pie so that when the idea and the concept were finally realized, there was nothing of your contribution left except the dot on the *i*.

Granted, she was working on a much larger scale with this account. And the stakes were high: millions of dollars, all costs told. But the aggravation, the secrecy, the constant humiliations were just not worth it for something so pie-in-the-sky.

And Global Vision was only one of ten agencies going through this first round. The client would then choose two campaigns it liked, and the face-off between the finalists would be continuing after that until the client made its choice. It was a six-month-to-a-year process, a merry-go-round that never ended; and then there was always another client, always another campaign.

She had her own work to do, and Carrie found herself sometimes wishing so hard that she could just have some time to think. There was no time for anything now but the client's concerns, the client's concept, the client's campaign.

No time, no time, no time.

She and the whole team were so sleep deprived, they

barely walked through the succeeding intense days. This wasn't creativity as she loved it. This was creation by committee, with every politically correct comma in place.

And she wished, in her heart of hearts, that she had never come to New York, because anybody with her experience could have sat in her place.

PORTLAND WAS about as big a city as Truck ever wanted to visit nowadays. New York was daunting. Huge. Enveloping, with those towering buildings everywhere you looked.

He liked a smaller scale, where a man could see where he was in relation to things. And in fact, he didn't know where he was in relation to Carrie, but enough was enough.

Truck intended to find out.

He didn't know the exact moment he decided to take Old Man's and Jeannie's advice and come to New York.

It might have been that he was damn tired of wrestling with his memories of the feel and heat of her that could not be exorcised by work and ruthless determination.

Or he might have decided that night he couldn't sleep, with every inch of his skin aching for just the touch of her hand.

Or it might have been that Old Man was right, and it was time to go after the warrior princess, capture her and bring her back to the castle.

A man lost patience sometimes waiting for results.

He had no particular plan. He just drove his van four hundred miles south one morning, with her motorcycle in the back. He hadn't even made a reservation anywhere; he arrived just about in time to check in for the night. And he found a hotel with valet parking, which was good because he knew nothing about the cutthroat parking rules in the city.

He was thinking straight, he thought as he checked in. He'd brought the cycle, surely an easier way to maneuver through the streets than trying to drive the van, and he was confronting his rival—the city and all it had to offer someone like Carrie.

And he had the name of the infernal agency: Jeannie had remembered it, and that night, he found the address in the phone book.

It wasn't going to be easy. Just from his first phone call to Global, asking for Carrie, and that cautious voice of the operator telling him she wasn't reachable, Truck knew he was going to need the strategy of an army general.

They made everything more important than it was and more difficult than it had to be.

He checked out the building. An innocuous white marble tower at the corner of Third Avenue and 52nd Street. People streaming in and out all day who all looked the same: slick and suited, with briefcases and laptop cases and perfect hair.

But he didn't see Carrie.

There was no phone listing for her, either so she hadn't rented an apartment or gotten a phone.

That made things harder.

That made him more determined.

And maybe it was as simple as storming the barricades, whatever they were. For some reason, her agency was hiding Carrie and everyone else working on the project that had brought her to New York.

He wondered what could be so all-damn important about it.

Well, it was time for a frontal assault.

He'd come on a Wednesday, reconnoitered on Thursday, and the following morning, he hitched himself onto the Harley and roared out into traffic.

He'd forgotten about the traffic, the jam-packed streets, the way you could only go a mile in about thirty minutes. But the nice thing about the Harley was you could zip down the avenues in between the lanes and avoid all that endless stopping and starting.

At nine o'clock precisely, he pulled the beast up onto the sidewalk in front of the Global Vision building, and rolled it into the lobby.

"But you can't," the guard protested.

"I'm going to," Truck said, and he must have looked so fierce, so wild and so menacing, the guard let him park there. "Where's Global?"

"Ten through fifteen."

Truck opted for floor fifteen, and when the elevator doors slid smoothly open, he stepped out into the bustle of the creative floor.

There were people streaming across the reception area in an endless do-si-do—in one door, cross the floor and out the other. There were sofas you could sink into and maybe disappear forever. Modern art on the walls, all slashes and bright colors.

And a receptionist who looked as if she might be helpful.

Or maybe not.

"Get Carrie Spencer." A tough voice, matched by a tough stance, it was the only way.

The receptionist picked up the phone. Dropped it. Couldn't keep her eyes off him. "Um, Carrie can't be reached."

"Reach her."

He could see she was waffling. "There's a big meeting upstairs today. I'm sure she's involved in it, and she won't be available until very late."

"Get her."

She punched in some numbers very fast, spoke in a low voice to whomever she reached on the other end and then looked up at him.

"Have a seat?"

"No. Is she coming?"

"They said they'll...um...send her right down."

"I'll wait by the elevator then."

"Right."

But what "they" meant by "right down" was wholly different from what he meant.

Damn them all. *They.* The mysterious, omnipotent *they...*

Ten minutes passed, fifteen... The receptionist was watching him warily. He must have looked dangerous, unstable. He felt that way.

Truck wheeled around to pin down the receptionist, and he saw her, coming from another direction, from behind the reception wall.

Leather and silk. That was Carrie. She looked thinner, or maybe he was hoping this project had been such a drain, she'd run into his arms, thankful to be rescued.

Fat chance. No, this was going to require drastic measures.

The receptionist pointed toward him.

Carrie turned, almost in slow motion, and she saw him walking purposefully toward her, dark, daring, dangerous. *There.*

Her breath caught. He had come for her. Come for *her.* It was the most breathtaking moment of her life. Her knees went weak, her heart started pounding wildly.

He had come for her at the very moment she needed to see him more than anything else in her life.

Hadn't she lived on the very memory of him? Hadn't she ached for him? Regretted every moment she'd spent away from him?

Been stupid and stubborn and wrongheaded about everything—including him?

Did it have to take three months away to make her understand all of that? And just what her feelings were for him?

She watched as he stalked toward her. He looked like an outlaw, as if he was coming to rescue his woman, and would never let her go.

Exactly what she wanted.

But he had always known exactly what she wanted...

He came toe to toe with her and she stood there, riveted by the sight of him and the obdurate expression on his face.

"We're going home."

This was not a moment to say *please, yes,* or *thank you.* Or to tell him she'd signed off on the project and out of the company—forever.

She just stood there, not saying a word, and he couldn't think of anything else to do but haul her up tightly against him and crush his mouth against hers.

"God almighty, tell me how I waited this long to kiss you again," he muttered against her lips, "because I sure the hell don't know."

"I don't either," she whispered, but he swallowed her words in his devouring kiss.

How had she lived all this time without that kiss?

She was vaguely aware that everyone was staring, and she didn't care.

The elevator dinged, the arrow pointing down, toward the moment of truth.

Truck wrenched his mouth from hers, and picked her up over his shoulder and marched inside.

"Are you crazy?" Carrie demanded as the doors closed to the sound of a faint spattering of applause.

He eased her down. "You're damn right I am. God, I am out of my mind for you." He cupped her face, and his mouth came down on hers, hard, hot, hungry. "I couldn't stand it anymore. God—Carrie..."

"Me neither," she murmured, feeling him shudder as she reached for him, ran her hands all over his face. "It was a stupid idea."

"Which? Your coming, or your going?"

He knew everything. "Going," she whispered. "I missed you, I did. I was counting the days, the minutes until I could get out of there. Don't stop. Truck, just don't stop..."

"I haven't stopped," he growled, his voice raspy. But he wanted to stop everything else, and just savor this moment.

He wanted to stop time.

The stop button was right by his hand. He pressed it firmly and the elevator jolted to a standstill.

Bells rang somewhere. Horns wailed.

He nudged his leg between hers. "How fast, how far?"

"How about across the street?" she whispered, nipping at his lips, touching him everywhere she could reach. "I don't have to be out of my hotel room till noon..."

"Only if you promise never to leave again." He backed her against the elevator wall, his body covering hers as tenaciously as if they were already in bed, as if he would keep her next to him forever.

Here was the heart and soul of his need for her, all the

heat, lust and desire, and she was ready, finally, for the ultimate surrender. She needed him too, and more than that, she wanted everything that he wanted, and everything he'd ever dreamed.

Carrie had no reservations now, she understood finally that there were never any guarantees, and the future would take care of itself.

And she meant to tell him that too. No more running. No more fighting her feelings. She was coming home for real, for good.

"Forget the hotel room," she whispered, melting against his strength and the rock-hard reality of him pressing against her.

"That could be arranged," he murmured, slanting his mouth over hers in an urgent stoking kiss that made them both writhe with its heat and its promise. "*What* did you say you're wearing under that skirt?"

"I'll let you find out..." She lost herself again in his grinding possessive kiss. She couldn't get enough of him; she was starved for him. She felt him nudging her, spreading her, smoothing his hand up her thigh, and she moved to ease his way.

A minute more and she would be connected to him for a lifetime.

They never heard the crackling of the speaker until a voice barked, "You okay up there?"

Truck groaned as he pulled a bare inch away from her lips. "Do we have to talk to him?"

"They'll send someone after us."

"We'll still have time to..."

"No, we have to tell him." Someone had to tell him, but Carrie wasn't sure she was in any shape to tell anyone anything. "We're okay," she called back, her voice quivering, her body quaking.

They couldn't get out of there soon enough, she thought fuzzily. Making love in the hotel room first. And the rest of their lives to follow.

It sounded like a plan to her.

The elevator began to move. She looked at Truck, who was looking a little dazed too. "*Are* we okay?"

He pulled her tightly against him.

"Actually," he murmured, "actually, I think we're in love."

Temptation®

COMING NEXT MONTH

EXTRA! EXTRA!

The book all your favorite authors are raving about is finally here!

The 1999 Harlequin and Silhouette coupon book.

Each page is alive with savings that can't be beat!

Getting this incredible coupon book is as easy as 1, 2, 3.

1. During the months of November and December 1999 buy any 2 Harlequin or Silhouette books.

2. Send us your name, address and 2 proofs of purchase (cash receipt) to the address below.

3. Harlequin will send you a coupon book worth $10.00 off future purchases of Harlequin or Silhouette books in 2000.

Send us 3 cash register receipts as proofs of purchase and we will send you 2 coupon books worth a total saving of $20.00 (limit of 2 coupon books per customer).

Saving money has never been this easy.

Please allow 4-6 weeks for delivery. Offer expires December 31, 1999.

I accept your offer! Please send me (a) coupon booklet(s):

Name: _____

Address: _____ City: _____

State/Prov.: _____ Zip/Postal Code: _____

Send your name and address, along with your cash register receipts as proofs of purchase, to:
In the U.S.: Harlequin Books, P.O. Box 9057, Buffalo, N.Y. 14269
In Canada: Harlequin Books, P.O. Box 622, Fort Erie, Ontario L2A 5X3

Order your books and accept this coupon offer through our web site
http://www.romance.net
Valid in U.S. and Canada only.

PHQ4994R